WITH THIS KISS

"I hate to leave." Prudence turned for one last, long look at London. "May I return someday?" she asked softly. "I like it up here. It seems we have spent many happy hours upon rooftops."

"That is true, Miss Reese. And I hope to spend many more." He hoped to have a lifetime of such happiness with her. And why not start with a kiss? She turned her lovely face to him, and he captured it between his hands.

"Oh!" Her lips parted.

"My dear Prudence! If I may—"

She knew what was coming and gave herself up, body and soul, to him.

BOOK YOUR PLACE ON OUR WEBSITE AND MAKE THE READING CONNECTION!

We've created a customized website just for our very special readers, where you can get the inside scoop on everything that's going on with Zebra, Pinnacle and Kensington books.

When you come online, you'll have the exciting opportunity to:

- View covers of upcoming books
- Read sample chapters
- Learn about our future publishing schedule (listed by publication month *and author*)
- Find out when your favorite authors will be visiting a city near you
- Search for and order backlist books from our online catalog
- Check out author bios and background information
- Send e-mail to your favorite authors
- Meet the Kensington staff online
- Join us in weekly chats with authors, readers and other guests
- Get writing guidelines
- AND MUCH MORE!

Visit our website at http://www.kensingtonbooks.com

THE PASSIONATE MISS PRUDENCE

Lisa Noeli

ZEBRA BOOKS
Kensington Publishing Corp.
www.kensingtonbooks.com

ZEBRA BOOKS are published by

Kensington Publishing Corp.
850 Third Avenue
New York, NY 10022

All Kensington titles, imprints and distributed lines are available at special quantity discounts for bulk purchases for sales promotion, premiums, fund-raising, educational or institutional use.

Special book excerpts or customized printings can also be created to fit specific needs. For details, write or phone the office of the Kensington Special Sales Manager: Kensington Publishing Corp., 850 Third Avenue, New York, NY 10022. Attn. Special Sales Department. Phone: 1-800-221-2647.

Zebra and the Z logo Reg. U.S. Pat. & TM Off.

First printing: January 2005
10 9 8 7 6 5 4 3 2 1

Printed in the United States of America

Chapter One

London, 1815

Books, books, books—heaps of them, hills of them, everywhere Prudence looked. In her opinion, not one was worth reading.

But her dear relation, Lady Agatha Purcell, did not think so. The old countess had scribbled approving comments in the one Prudence was looking through now. *My thoughts precisely. Sage words indeed.* And the ultimate accolade . . . *How true!*

Lady Agatha had underlined the last two words three times.

Evidently she thought highly of this book of advice for young gentlewomen. Its right reverend author was renowned for his fire-and-brimstone sermons on the ever-popular subject of Lust.

He ought to know, Prudence thought. The London scandal sheets had made the most of the story of a Miss Tipton, a pretty chambermaid in the reverend's employ, reporting her spirited defense of her virtue with a coal scuttle and the astounding size of the resulting lump on his noggin.

Not that Lady Agatha would ever believe such tittle-tattle. The good old lady considered him a dear friend and often consulted him on spiritual matters, reprobate though he was—and the Right Reverend Chester Ponsonby had signed the title page, penning a dedication with an inky flourish.

From Oysters of Knowledge Come Pearls of Wisdom! The very words that Lady Agatha wanted inscribed upon the cornerstone of her library, Prudence knew, with an oyster rampant upon a field of pearls.

She clapped the book shut and waved away a small cloud of dust. Evidently no young gentlewoman had bothered to take the vicar's advice for some time.

Smiling, Prudence opened another worthy volume. She had only herself to blame. Founding a lending library for women had been her suggestion, but she had not expected Lady Agatha to take to it with such zeal.

The old lady, impulsive by nature, thought it a capital way to spend her late husband's considerable fortune. It was certainly more practical than her last crack-brained attempt at free education, Prudence thought.

Perhaps instructing South Sea islanders on the glorious history of England, including parliamentary procedure and the fine points of sheep shearing, had seemed like a good idea at the time. And Lady Agatha's noble friends had cleared their shelves of dusty volumes on these and other subjects, sending waggons heaped high with them to the docks as ballast for the good ship *Wisdom.*

Much to the captain's indignation, the South Sea islanders proved to be unable to read—a small detail that Lady Agatha had not thought of—and ultimately refused this gracious gift. They had then commandeered the vessel's store of rum at the point of a hundred spears.

The rejected volumes were accidentally thrown

overboard on the return voyage by the crew—to make room for a cargo of pigs and pineapples, the captain explained once safely back in England. He had humbly begged her ladyship's pardon.

Undaunted, Lady Agatha was amassing books once more—and to repay her distant relation's many kindnesses, Prudence was attempting to catalogue at least a thousand titles, some old, some new.

It was assumed, as Prudence was unmarried, that she had nothing better to do. She certainly could not refuse to help, since Lady Agatha had been so kind as to sponsor Prudence's first season, with an eye to an advantageous match.

But the project of the library seemed to interest the old lady much more. Its walls were rising fast—in fact, it was being built not a stone's throw away. Prudence could hear the masons and bricklayers cursing from the third floor room where she sat.

Though she could not yet see the walls, the massive, square-cut timbers holding the block and tackle that lifted bricks, lumber, and mortar were just visible above the neighboring roof.

Less than a year ago, Lady Agatha had contrived to purchase an old tavern and stables near her new but not completed house in a somewhat unfashionable section of London. The ramshackle structures were razed and the ground cleared before she asked her second son, Lord Purcell, to serve as architect for the library. He agreed somewhat reluctantly, according to his mother, as her town house—this house, which he had also designed—was not quite finished.

Prudence wondered how he was able to design two such complicated projects at once—*and* satisfy the odd and constantly changing whims of his widowed mama. He must be a busy man indeed, for she had yet to see him in the flesh, though she had come down to London months ago.

Apparently, Lord Alwyn also had numerous social obligations, or so said his valet, who liked to brag belowstairs of his master's huncommon talent for romantical conquests. His full-length portrait in the front hall of Purcell House, placed there by his doting mama, certainly looked romantical enough.

She did not know whether any of it was true but the valet was not the only one who liked to talk.

This gossip had reached Prudence's ears thanks to Liz, her ladies' maid, a fount of information, recently sacked by Lady Agatha for cooing over this portrait with unseemly enthusiasm.

The artist had made Lord Alwyn Purcell look remarkably handsome, with a proud air. His hair was black and wavy, and his eyes, a limpid and unstable green. His nose was Roman and his lips were slightly full.

According to Liz, who had heard it from other ladies' maids, the *ton* belles exclaimed over his sensual good looks and twittered about him endlessly at teas.

Prudence avoided such occasions, which had given her an unwelcome and unwarranted reputation as a bluestocking. Apparently she was thought to be too clever—and Lady Agatha had not reassured her by saying that anyone with half a brain could be considered too clever by those with none.

It was an odd comment coming from a real bluestocking, but that was Lady Agatha for you. She spoke first and thought afterwards.

Prudence rose from her chair and kicked a stack of books with a blue-and-white striped silk slipper, watching them topple into one of the winding paths she had made through the heaps.

She walked to the looking-glass that hung between the drawing room windows and surveyed her reflection, brushing off dust from her dress. At least her face was clean.

As usual, she looked like herself—to her eyes, unexceptional in every way. Her light brown hair had an annoying tendency to curl in all directions; her eyes were blue; her cheeks, pink; her nose, small.

She smoothed her light blue dress, regretting its overly modest cut. Such womanly charms as she possessed were not shown to advantage—not that there was anyone to admire them.

The door opened of a sudden, and Prudence nearly jumped. Behind her in the glass was none other than Lord Alwyn Purcell! He seemed not to have noticed her.

She turned to face him, thinking that he ought to have knocked before entering. Then she reminded herself that this was more his domain than hers. His mother had told her that, though he kept his own apartments in London, he stayed occasionally at Purcell House, since the site of the future library was so near.

He still had not noticed Prudence, who watched him dash to the huge walnut desk against the opposite wall, pulling open its many drawers, sometimes two at once, as if he were looking for something he valued highly and had lost.

Prudence shrank back slightly, wishing the gold silk drapery at the window would swallow her and wondering what it was he sought.

"Hell's bells! Where are those drawings? I will be in no end of trouble if I cannot find—well, well."

He pushed back a lock of black hair that had fallen into his eyes and glowered at her. "What are you doing here and who are you?"

"I am Prudence Reese, your very distant—cousin, I think. I am staying with your mother for the season. We are choosing appropriate titles for her lending library." She began edging toward the door, knowing that Lady Agatha, though not a stickler for propriety, might take it amiss if they were alone together for long.

Lord Alwyn looked distractedly at the heaps of books.

"Ah, yes, of course. Mama did mention that a young relation, a young woman—I suppose she meant you—would be staying here for some weeks. Well, have you read any?" His arched eyebrow and haughty tone seemed to imply that doing so would be a very great waste of time, but Prudence could not be sure.

"I have just looked through *Lessons for Modest Misses*—the Reverend Ponsonby's book. Perhaps you have read it." Prudence blushed, suddenly feeling foolish.

Lord Alwyn shot her a killing look. "Indeed I have not. Filthy old fellow. Mama thinks most highly of Ponsonby, however. I have refrained from disillusioning her."

Prudence wanted to laugh. So the rumors were true—or least Lord Alwyn thought they were. "I see."

"Mama collects clergymen the way she collects bric-a-brac." He waved a hand at the bizarre furniture that crowded the room. "There seems to be no stopping her."

"Indeed." Prudence nodded in polite agreement.

Lady Agatha's son might criticize the old lady's taste, but it was not Prudence's place to do so.

"Miss Reese, I have mislaid some drawings. I know they are not in my own apartments, for I have ransacked those from top to bottom. I don't suppose you have seen them?" He shook his head, as if to clear his befuddled brain. "Oh—do forgive me. You would not know what I mean. They are not at all the sort of drawings that a young lady might have in her possession."

An impatient male voice hallooed up the stairs, bidding him to make haste.

"I am coming!" Lord Alwyn roared back.

Prudence winced. She was tempted to reprimand him for hurting her ears but she told herself that his impressive roar was perhaps only natural for an architect, who had to be heard from the street to the very top of a building scaffold.

He banged all but one of the drawers closed as vigorously as he had opened them.

"Damnation! Where the devil have those drawings gone?" He stopped and looked up, studying her for a moment. "Miss Reese, forgive my ill temper—you are quivering with fear."

"I have no fear of you, sir," she replied pertly. "But your voice is too loud for this small room. You gave me a start, that is all."

The male voice called out again, and Lord Alwyn slammed the last drawer shut. On his finger.

Prudence thought it best to depart at once.

Chapter Two

Prudence heard a great noise of boots coming downstairs seconds later, along with some remarkably inventive oaths. She ducked into a high niche meant for a statue that had yet to be installed. She closed her eyes and drew a deep breath, letting it out when the boots stopped.

"You!"

Her eyes flew open. Lord Alwyn was standing directly in front of her, breathing rather heavily. He pointed a finger at her and she saw that the nail was bruised blue.

"Oh, dear," she began but he interrupted her.

"You distracted me." He let out a prodigious sigh. "Well, never mind. You are a very pretty woman, Miss Reese. I suppose you could not help it."

She averted her gaze from his broad chest, which was clad in immaculate linen and a sober waistcoat. "Indeed, sir, your injury is no fault of mine. Now if you will permit me to pass, I shall return to my work."

He did not budge an inch but only looked at her as if taking her measure. "I intended to put a statue of Diana in that very niche, you know, when I designed this house."

He continued to study her in a most disquieting

way. Prudence was silent, having no idea what he might say or do next.

"But you will do nicely in Diana's stead. You greatly resemble the goddess who hunts by moonlight and your figure is as perfect—"

"You are talking perfect nonsense, Lord Alwyn," Prudence said severely. "Let me pass."

He bowed somewhat stiffly, as if playing a gentleman on stage, but he did not step aside. "Forgive me, Miss Reese. Meeting you was a most pleasant surprise, but when I could not find those damned drawings—oh, forgive me. I should not swear as much as I do. Mama detests it."

"Prooo-dence!" This agitated tremolo belonged to Lady Agatha.

"She is here, Mama!" Lord Alwyn called. "We are discussing classical statuary." He still had not moved and Prudence was effectively trapped.

"Alwyn! Do not engage in idle banter with Miss Reese! Her assistance is of critical importance if the library is to open on schedule. The young women of London must be served!"

"Indeed they must," he called down, grinning wolfishly. Then he whispered for Prudence's benefit, "No doubt there will be throngs of nubile females, eager for moral guidance. I cannot wait to observe the spectacle."

"Oh, that is enough!" She put her hands to his chest and pushed him aside, then stopped, looking up into his green eyes. Had she felt—just for one delightful second—the beating of a strong male heart? The sensation was much more disconcerting than his indiscreet jests.

He scarcely seemed to notice her action and moved quickly to look over the rail at his concerned parent far below—and something else. "Oh!" He turned back to her. "Perhaps I left the drawings in the chiffomonster. I did not think to look there."

"The chiffo-what?"

"You know, that colossal thing in the hall." He looked at her suspiciously. "You must have noticed it. Hooks for hats, pigeonholes for bills, drawers for gloves, cabinets for boots, and a full-length glass for admiring oneself? Mama found it secondhand in a shop on Tottenham Court Road."

"Oh, that. I did not know it was called a chiffomonster."

"That is what I call it, Miss Reese."

"I see. Well, your mother thinks it is beautiful. And it does hold a great many useful items."

Lord Alwyn sniffed. "I should not be surprised to find a litter of rabbits in one of its compartments. It is an eyesore."

Lady Agatha, who was plump, essayed the first step far below and stopped then and there, wheezing mightily. "Alwyn! Your disreputable friend is waiting! I will not countenance rudeness! Come down at once!"

He looked over the banister railing at his motionless parent and waved to her. "Please calm yourself, Mama. Miss Reese and I will be down shortly."

"How shortly?" Lady Agatha's voice vibrated with ferocious intensity. "Alwyn, your reputation is such that—" The rest was lost in a fit of coughing.

"Within seconds!"

Lady Agatha wheezed.

He winked at Prudence, who had almost forgotten that she still stood in the niche, and spoke too softly for his mother to hear.

"Good-bye, Miss Reese. I shall join you and Mama

this evening if I can. I must warn you that she dines with diamonds on and you will be expected to dress for the occasion. Therefore, allow me to remove this trace of dust." He brushed a warm hand over her cheek as if he could not resist doing so. "There. Though you are lovely even with it."

Startled beyond measure, Prudence put her own hand to her face. She had noticed no such trace of dust when she had inspected her reflection in the mirror. Clearly, Lord Alwyn was an incorrigible flirt and undoubtedly deserved the reputation his mother had mentioned.

Oh! Wonder of wonders, he placed an audacious kiss—the merest brush of his lips, but still—upon the cheek that he had caressed, then hoisted himself upon the smooth banister and slid out of sight.

The next voice Prudence heard was Lady Agatha's.

"Alwyn! You are displaying a regrettable lack of dignity—it will never do—and the banister has just been polished!"

"Then I have polished it again, Mama."

Prudence heard a noise of more drawers and doors opening and shutting as he ransacked the chiffomonster, looking for his drawings.

"Damnation! They are not here either!"

Prudence looked down the stairwell and saw Lord Alwyn bestow a hasty embrace upon his mother before he dashed out the door.

Thank heavens Lady Agatha had not seen his indescribably tender gesture—or that playful kiss. No doubt the dowager countess planned a brilliant match for her vigorous second son.

It was common knowledge that her first, Eugene, on whom the title of earl was entirely wasted, was in poor health, fond of strong drink, and never left his country house. But if Prudence were to marry Alwyn—

Where had *that* extremely odd idea come from? Just because Lord Purcell happened to stumble over her in his mad rush down the stairs and then said some very silly but nonetheless gallant things and then offered a caress, surely without thinking . . . all that meant nothing.

Prudence scolded herself silently for letting her imagination run riot. She arranged her skirts and composed herself, then went downstairs in a trembling hurry to assist her benefactress.

Lord Alwyn ran down the front stairs, seeking the man who had called to him, now some yards away in the street, talking to his coachman.

"Charles! Do wait for me!" Lord Alwyn covered the distance with long strides to stand beside his friend and fellow architect, Charles Sudbury. "We must find the drawings for the reading room dome or construction cannot proceed. It is extremely important that the outer walls are properly strengthened to support it!"

"My dear Alwyn, I have them here in my hand. Whatever are you going on about?" Charles held up a tubular drawing case made of leather and rapped his friend gently on the head with it.

Lord Alwyn sighed with relief. "Devil take you! And I thought I had lost them for good."

"You are distracted of late. Are you in love, my dear fellow? Come, we must be off." The gentlemen swung themselves up into the carriage and settled back against the squabs. Charles gave Alwyn a measuring look. "Tell me—who is the enchantress and how has she cast her spell?"

Alwyn stared out the cloudy little window at the passersby and hawkers. This part of London was crowded and the streets were narrow. "There is no enchantress, Charles."

"An opera dancer perhaps? A tavern wench of splendid proportions?"

"Do not indulge in idle speculation, if you please. It has a way of turning into rumor, and from that into what 'everyone knows.' I am a very busy man, Charles, and I have neither the time nor the inclination for romantic entanglements."

"Piffle. My sweet Jenny says that you have a reputation as a rake."

Alwyn snorted. "Well, I have never embraced her, at least."

Charles yawned.

Alwyn knew it was whispered that Jenny, who called herself an actress, had other admirers and that Charles did not care.

"Frederick Sills said your mother had invited a distant relation to stay for the season," Charles persisted. "A Miss Reese, is it? He and his wife saw the gel out walking with your mother."

"Yes. Well, Mama is in charge of her coming-out, I believe. She is a modest miss, and eminently respectable."

"Fred said she was a pretty thing."

"Did he." Alywn's tone was flat, as he wished not to explain further.

"Yes. He did. Confess, old friend. Are you smitten with her?"

"No. I have only just met her today, Charles. You know that I am not often at home. Mama and her endless parade of clerics do not make the most entertaining company."

Charles only harrumphed in reply. Alwyn fell silent, thinking of Miss Reese. Her spirited charm made her far more than pretty. She was flowerlike, in the first bloom of her young womanhood, positively dewy—*stop it*, he told himself.

Even if he had given in to a mad impulse only minutes ago, caressed her petal-soft cheek and kissed her ever so briefly, he would not share that information with Charles, who liked to gossip.

But how could a chit like Prudence Reese make him feel, for a few giddy seconds, like a lovestruck lad of nineteen? He was a grown man of thirty-one with too many responsibilities and not enough time. But he had enjoyed that glorious feeling, damn it all.

Odd that she had inspired it. He preferred women of a more worldly nature as a rule, who understood that he was not a marrying man and who parted from him with scarcely a tear—women who were as unwilling to be bound by love as he was.

Love—he would have to admit, if pressed, that he really knew nothing about it. Alwyn stared absently out the carriage window.

Charles was more right than he knew. Miss Prudence Reese *was* an enchantress, despite her modest dress and demure manners. Her porcelain skin and sylphlike figure needed no daringly diaphanous gown to be shown to advantage. And her features were flawless.

"Bother," he said, not realizing that he was speaking until it was too late.

"What?" inquired Charles.

"Nothing. I was thinking aloud." He compressed

his lips and vowed not to do that again. Once Charles had the least inkling that Miss Reese had stirred up such emotions, the questions would begin.

Though she might be more beautiful and certainly more intelligent than most—not to mention grace-ful—and impertinent—and utterly charming—Alwyn would not commence a dalliance with her.

No doubt Miss Reese hoped to find a rich husband and his mama was helping her in this endeavor. But Alwyn, though a gentleman, would never lead a life of leisure—such was the fate of a younger son.

His architectural training had brought him some lucrative commissions, but not wealth. Not yet. He would need a few impossibly rich patrons with a pas-sion for building mansions of mind-boggling size.

At the rate his wastrel brother was going through the family fortune, it would be well and truly pissed away before Eugene managed to kill himself with drink.

Fortunately or unfortunately, depending on one's point of view, their mother's inheritance was held in complex trusts and would revert to the male relatives on her side without a penny going to her offspring. The money his father had left Lady Agatha might go to the unscrupulous clergymen who fawned over her, Alwyn thought grimly.

Hardly the sort of family an innocent like Miss Reese would want to marry into. Clearly his mother intended her to wed some blameless fellow with twenty thousand pounds per annum free and clear.

It stood to reason, since Mama had often voiced her hopes to marry him off to an heiress with a sim-ilar income and a liking for children. Eugene had produced none, despite his numerous liaisons.

His brother had no wife, did not want one, and

avoided his do-gooding mother at every opportunity, leaving it to Alwyn to see that she was happy. Agreeing to build her library had already cost him a fat fee. A wealthy and impatient brewer in need of a sprawling country house for his ever-growing family had gone to someone else.

But the world was full of parvenus, Alwyn reflected. An unknown in the jostling crowd upon the street outside might become rich overnight, given the English thirst for ale.

"You are thoughtful, my friend." Charles looked at him shrewdly. "I still say there is a woman on your mind."

Lord Alwyn smiled, ready at last to concede the point. "Perhaps."

"Hm. But you will not say which one."

"No."

Charles shrugged. "Well, you will meet your match someday. I expect you will know the moment it happens."

"The moment *what* happens? Do not be cryptic, Charles."

"You know perfectly well, my good fellow. Love."

"Oh, that."

Alwyn looked out the window again, seeing a young woman who looked a little like Miss Reese, there upon the cobblestones, twirling a parasol.

The resemblance was very slight. But it was proof enough that she was on his mind, even if the poor girl was undoubtedly still at home, dusting dull books for his mama.

He tried to remember precisely what that dear lady had said about Miss Reese before her arrival and drew a blank. It didn't matter. Young women came to London for one reason, and that was to find a husband.

Obviously, once out, she would have more than her share of eager dancing partners at balls and assemblies and so forth—and she would not want for distinguished suitors.

He looked at Charles, who had opened a pocket-size novel with salacious engravings and was studying it closely, thus saving Alwyn the trouble of further conversation.

He fell into a reverie once more. Certainly he would be delighted to dance with Miss Reese. He imagined her reaching up to rest her soft hand upon his shoulder while he took the other and led her in a waltz.

In better clothes, she would be acclaimed as a diamond of the first water. Not that he particularly noticed feminine fripperies, except to confirm his theory that the most lackwitted females usually had the most lavish gowns.

A vague memory from several weeks ago came to mind: his mother happily confiding that Prudence was a bit of a bluestocking. Having seen her at last, Alwyn very much doubted it.

The intelligent fire in her eyes intrigued him most. She had not seemed to care a fig when he compared her—rather elegantly, he thought—to the goddess Diana. A more conventional young lady would have simpered and affected the sort of feminine airs that always annoyed him. But Prudence had only pushed him aside impatiently.

He remembered the feel of her hands upon his chest for those few seconds with pleasure—he had not expected her to behave so boldly. Evidently Miss Reese did not like to feel cornered. He made a mental note of that interesting fact, as the wheels clattered over the cobblestones toward Charles's club.

Prudence waited patiently as Lady Agatha took each step, giving the old lady her arm and murmurs of encouragement.

"My dear girl!" Lady Agatha paused upon the second landing, wheezing again. "Stairs are a trial indeed for those who are neither slender nor young. I cannot get my breath, even though I have given up my corsets. Do you know, Reverend Ponsonby found no mention of them in the Bible."

"Oh?" Prudence said. She wondered why he expected to in the first place.

"He says women ought to follow the example of their ancient foremothers and walk about unconstrained."

From what little she knew of Ponsonby, Prudence did not wonder at that.

"Onward!" Lady Agatha puffed. "We must review the books we have at hand. Mark my words, no unwholesome romances or tales of horror will make their way into the collection. I mean to improve the minds of women, strengthen their characters—that sort of thing."

Prudence, who disliked, on principle, books that were said to be improving, said nothing in reply. They continued up, propelled by Lady Agatha's bottomless determination to do good.

"Prudence, have you dusted the older volumes? I cannot—my weak lungs will not permit me such exertions, even for the betterment of womankind."

"Yes, I have. Most of them." Prudence brought a

hand to her cheek, to the spot where Lord Alwyn had so tenderly brushed away the imaginary smudge. She would happily dust a very mountain of books if he would do that once more.

"Very good. The housemaids cannot be trusted with the task, except for Cathy, who is a bright girl." She patted Prudence's hand. "I thought she might do as your lady's maid, my dear, now that Liz is gone. She might do for both of us, now that I do not need to be laced up."

"Of course, Lady Agatha. Whatever you think."

"You need someone to see to your dresses and coiffures. You must not concern yourself with petty things. Dear Prudence, I expect you could do anything you put your mind to. You might even have a calling."

"Yes, Lady Agatha." Prudence could not imagine what her old relation was thinking. As the last of the Reese children, her education had been haphazard at best, with an emphasis on art and music but only a dash of arithmetic.

If Prudence had to say what interested her most, it would be people—they were endlessly fascinating. But that did not count as a calling.

"What remains to be done, my dear?"

"There are boxes of books just lately come from Mr. Furnivall's shop, the ones he could not sell. Broderick carried them upstairs."

"We must inspect them all for suitable content— a tedious task. But virtue is its own reward. If we heed the uplifting advice of Reverend Ponsonby . . ." The old lady prattled on.

Prudence did not interrupt, though her suspicion that Ponsonby had uplifted more skirts than minds had been confirmed by Lord Alwyn.

In due time, they gained the upper story and walked into the sunny room.

The winding paths Prudence had made between the heaps of books now proved useful to aid Lady Agatha's progress to her son's desk.

The old lady collapsed into the sturdy chair behind it and sighed happily. "So many! They will look very fine on the shelves, I think, when the library is completed."

"Indeed, ma'am," Prudence said respectfully.

"I see that you have done a great deal, my dear. At some point we must alphabetize them. A is for apple and all that—and oh! Applegate! Speak of the devil!"

She waved a wrinkled hand and laughed, pleased with her little joke. "Alwyn mentioned that Bishop Applegate had given him a signed copy of his new book, *Moral Discourses*. The dear boy swore he would use it for kindling, but I am sure he has not. Anyway, not yet."

Prudence smiled politely as the old lady rattled on. "If you could find the volume—it is rather small—perhaps I will read aloud while you open the boxes from Furnivall's."

She could pretend to look for it, Prudence thought, and make it disappear if she was so unlucky as to find it in the tumbled heaps. Prudence had heard Bishop Applegate hold forth at length for several Sundays in a row. The man explained every possible sin—including several that the fashionably amoral congregation had not even thought of—as the fault of Eve alone, exempting Adam of all blame. It was most annoying.

She made a great show of searching and happened to spy the small book on the floor. Lady

Agatha, who was nearsighted, did not. Prudence hastily kicked it underneath the desk with the tip of her shoe.

"Dear Lady Agatha, perhaps you should rest instead. Do not strain yourself by reading."

The old lady nodded and rose to her feet, holding on to the desk for support. "I am quite tired. Still, I did want to see what quantity we had thus far and I am pleased indeed. If you will assist me to the divan, my dear Prudence, I shall rest as you suggest."

Once settled into the sprigged silk cushions, Lady Agatha relaxed visibly. The warmer atmosphere of the uppermost floor seemed to make her sleepy and the polished brass clock ticking on the mantle did the rest. It was not long before the old lady dozed off.

Prudence resumed her work, selecting a box and carefully separating the pages of the new books with a knife for that purpose she found on Lord Alwyn's desk.

It was a tedious task, as Lady Agatha had said, and the new books were no more exciting than the old. There were collections of dry sermons, and vehement broadsides on feminine deportment and etiquette that scarcely seemed to deserve the dignity of gold-embossed bindings, and pompous philosophies, all in very small print—and all written by men, Prudence noted. Angry, narrow-minded men.

She soldiered on.

Some hours and many boxes later, now sitting upon the intricately patterned carpet, Prudence pulled out a final book, bound in scarlet leather. It seemed rather different from the others, more inviting in appearance, at the very least, though she knew only too well not to judge these books by their covers. She opened it.

Prudence looked at the title page: *The Persuasion of Pamela Jones*. The author was anonymous—and female, judging by the silhouette printed upon the frontispiece.

Her curiosity was piqued. Who was the fictional Pamela and what had she been persuaded to do?

Chapter Three

Prudence read for several minutes and skimmed the rest, noting the shoddy printing and the ungrammatical prose. Though the author hinted at fascinating sins, there were so many dashes and ellipses that it was nearly impossible to make sense of the narrative.

Snowy bosoms heaved and strong men sighed—but once the bedside candle was blown out and the hero and heroine plunged into darkness, exactly what they were up to was not clear. Which was just as well.

Prudence was troubled enough by her thoughts of the impetuous and rakishly handsome Lord Alwyn. She closed the scarlet-bound book firmly and stuffed it into a box of discards, thinking that she could write a much better romance if she had the time and inclination.

Perhaps that was her calling. It might be as good a way as any to make a bit of money. She would not have to use her real name and no one need know. How and where to begin—that was something she would have to find out. She could not very well ask Lady Agatha.

She stretched this way and that, easing the stiffness of her position upon the floor, and thought it over.

Her childhood on a distant country estate had been spent in tomboyish pursuits, not poring over books, even if a succession of governesses had tactfully described her as quick to learn. She would have to study this one more closely. She pulled the red book out of the box of discards and slipped it under the divan for further perusal at a later date.

Though she had not touched the sleeper upon the yellow silk upholstery, Lady Agatha snorted and rolled over rather clumsily, losing one shoe as she did so.

Prudence picked it up and carefully put it back onto the old lady's dangling foot. Lady Agatha snorted again.

She held her breath but the old lady did not awaken. The afternoon sunlight had made the room still warmer.

Yawning, Prudence reclined in an unladylike way upon the carpet. There was no one to see her do it.

In this position, she could just reach the small book she had kicked under the desk. Perhaps it would be best if Bishop Applegate's *Discourses* went into the box of discards sooner rather than later, underneath the others where Lady Agatha would not see it. She stretched out a hand and picked it up.

Several pages came loose—drawings of some sort. A Rake's Progress? Undoubtedly added to illustrate the moral lessons of the dismal text, Prudence thought. She rolled over upon her front to look at the drawings more closely.

They had been done with a miniaturist's skill, in the sweetly mannered style of the French masters. Delicate strokes of pen and ink depicted an amorous couple dallying in a garden. The sketched figures were fully clothed, but the tenderness that the artist had captured between them made it clear that they were in love.

She sighed. Ought she to keep them? And where could she hide them safe from prying eyes? They were certainly not at all the sort of drawings that a young lady might have in her possession—

Were those not Lord Alwyn's very words? Were they what he had looked for so eagerly? Prudence hastily stuffed the drawings back into the book and put it where she could easily find it later.

Lord Alwyn studied the plans for his mother's library, looking up at a halloo from a workman, who waved at him cheerfully from atop the half-completed walls and scaffolding. The rickety structure of poles and planks held a quantity of bricks and it seemed wise not to walk underneath.

Charles, rather the worse for the wine he had consumed at an excellent midday meal, had no such fears and walked about willy-nilly. His boots were muddy and his close-cut coat of superfine bore splotches of mortar and dust.

"I say, Alwyn, let's have a look at those drawings. Shomething is wrong"—he hiccupped—"those walls don't look quite shtraight to me."

Lord Alwyn gave him a dry look. He trusted the considerable experience of the workmen, and Herrick, his master builder and fellow freemason, more than his inebriated friend. "Nothing looks straight to you, Charles, because you are tipsy."

Charles peered at him with half-closed eyes. "So I am. Blame the burgundy. Or was it the brandy?"

"Stick to good old English ale, my friend. It will not addle your wits."

Charles nodded. "An exshellent idea. Where has my coachman gone? I shall have him drive me to an alehouse immediately."

"Very well. I shall remain here." Lord Alywn examined the structure and scaffolding thoughtfully, rubbing his chin.

"I tell you the walls are crooked! You must meash—you must measure."

"If only there was some way to rise to the top and survey the whole structure!"

"Climb the shcaffold." Charles had already attempted to do so, and had been gently led away by the foreman.

"I want to be above it, Charles."

"Then have the men hoist you up with the block and tackle. That is how Sir Christopher Wren got a good look at St. Paul's Cathedral when it was a-building and that was almost a shentury ago."

"I am a great admirer of that architect, but I have no wish to be hoisted, as you put it."

"Then you are a coward, sir. Wren rode up in a bloody great basket to the very top of the dome. And never was there a finer edifish!" Charles pulled himself up to his full height and assumed the booming tone of a country parson. "Never was there a finer edifish built by mortal man for the glory of our God!"

"Thank you for those noble sentiments, Charles."

"And it hasn't fallen down yet," Charles added, rather more practically. His knees wobbled and he leaned heavily against Alwyn.

"No, but you might. Allow me to walk to your coach." Lord Alwyn planned to instruct the coachman *sotto voce*, once Charles was safely sprawled inside, to take him home at once.

When the carriage rattled away, Lord Alwyn returned to the construction site. The foreman undoubtedly knew where such a conveyance could be found, and the block and tackle was not presently in use. He explained his requirement to Herrick, who dispatched a 'prentice and a waggon to Billingsgate at once.

The 'prentice returned with a bloody great basket in less than an hour. Lord Alwyn looked it over rather nervously. Clearly, it had been recently used to carry fish—a great deal of fish—and it still smelled of brine.

"Herrick, how strong is this?"

"Held fifteen stone of haddock, sir. Very fresh haddock it were. We could take ye back to Billingsgate and put ye 'pon the fishmonger's scales, just t' be safe."

"Well, I daresay I weigh less than that." Lord Alwyn had no intention of making a spectacle of himself in a public marketplace. "Go ahead then. Rig it with the strongest rope you have."

"Very good, sir." Herrick called the foreman over and it was not long before the huge basket was swinging over the platform from which the bricks and mortar were loaded. The bricklayers and stonemasons atop the walls gathered to watch and shout occasional words of advice.

The foreman tipped the basket so that Lord Alwyn might enter. He clambered inside rather awkwardly, stood up straight and clutched the rim, summoning up all the dignity he could muster. The men cheered lustily and he felt a little better, despite the powerful smell of haddock.

He gave what he hoped was an appropriate signal. The rope holders gave a mighty pull and the basket lurched left and then right. Lord Alwyn's stomach lurched with it. They pulled harder and he swung free of the platform, hanging several feet in the air.

The watching men cheered again. Alwyn waved to them but clutched the rim even more tightly with his other hand.

A cheeky sparrow alighted for a moment on the basket's rim and gave him a surprised look. Clearly, it thought humans belonged on the ground, not in midair. Alwyn had to agree.

The little bird flew away as the brawny fellows manning the rope pulled hand over hand, straining with the effort. Alywn soon cleared the top of the half-built walls. They seemed straight enough from this elevation but he could not be certain without careful measurements and due calculations upon those.

Thunk. He had reached the top of the massive timber that supported the block and tackle.

From this vantage point, he had an excellent view of the ever-growing city of London and the not too distant Thames. He heard the men below secure the pulling rope, following Herrick's shouted directions.

Of all things—he could see his mother's house quite clearly—well, if the basket would stop revolving, he could. He held tightly to its rim, feeling slightly ill.

In a minute or two, if the accursed basket would cease its dizzying rotation, he could look about—perhaps even attempt to measure key points upon the half-built walls. He felt about his person. Damnation. In all the excitement, he had neglected to bring his pocket instruments, or pencil and paper, or anything of use.

He wondered what Icarus had forgotten in his

flight to the sun, besides that he ought not to emulate the gods.

A slight breeze ruffled his hair, reviving his spirits a little. He turned as slowly as he could, so as not to rock the basket, and his mother's house came into view once more. A window on the top story was open—and out of it leaned Miss Prudence Reese, her pretty mouth wide open with surprise.

"Lord Alwyn!" Her voice was faint but it carried on the breeze.

He half-glimpsed his mother, asleep on the yellow divan. Really, he thought, his dear mama could fall asleep anywhere. But if *she* were to suddenly awake and see him swinging from a rope at this height, she undoubtedly would be frightened out of her wits.

He put his finger over his lips to indicate that Prudence should be silent, but the small gesture seemed to be lost on her.

Then he waved with both hands, not wanting to shout and wake his mother, hoping that Prudence might somehow read his mind. The basket began to revolve again, faster this time, and he felt very queasy indeed. He sat down inside it.

So much for the scenic panorama of the ever-growing city of London. At the moment all he could see were the woven withes of the basket's sides . . . and that was all he wanted to see.

"Hallo!" That was Herrick's booming voice. "Should we lower you now, sir?"

He clambered unsteadily to his feet. "Yes, thank you." He looked down at Herrick, who seemed impossibly small. "I have made the necessary measurements," he lied.

"Very good, sir."

The basket revolved once more, and Lord Alwyn

saw Prudence at the window. She pointed to his mother, who was—thank heavens—still sleeping soundly. He gave Prudence a debonair smile, as if he did things like this all the time, though he swore inwardly that he would never do it again.

The men below loosened the hitch that held the rope, and Alwyn felt a sickening drop. To distract himself, he counted the number of bones he was likely to break if he fell, and divided it by the doctor's probable fee.

He looked at Prudence. Her hands were clasped. Were her lips moving? He could not be sure. If she was praying, it was most kind of her to intercede with the Almighty on his behalf.

He murmured a few words from a half-remembered psalm himself, promising to atone for his many sins at some unspecified point in the future. There was no sense in overdoing it. Lord Alywn prided himself on being a rational man.

He felt the basket lower at last and he heaved a tremendous sigh of relief as he sank below the top of the scaffold, waving to the admiring workmen as if his brief aerial voyage had been nothing to him at all.

But the bump of landing was the final insult to his stomach, which felt as if it were still on high. Herrick assisted him from the basket, and Lord Alwyn staggered over to the mortar pit, where he puked.

To his amazement, when he wiped his mouth and stood up straight, the workmen gave him the loudest cheers of all.

Several hours later . . .

It felt very odd to be sneaking past a half-open door at his age, Lord Alwyn reflected. Yet the muffled clink of silver and china told him that dinner had been served. He had no wish to explain his late arrival or his vile-smelling clothes to his mother.

The sweet ring of feminine chatter filled the air, along with the tempting aromas of the evening repast. Two of his favorite things, certainly—food and females—but he did not dare stop.

The door swung open all the way, and the new serving maid traipsed out, jauntily swinging a silver basket of rolls. She was a pleasant-faced girl with thick red hair—was her name Catherine or Cathy? He could not remember. His mother had praised her modesty and quick thinking, he knew that much.

Whatever her name, the maid was followed by Mrs. Dawkins, the cook, who clutched a majolica tureen to her ample bosom. Though far too prone to talk of scandal, which his mother blamed upon the cheap newspapers Mrs. Dawkins adored, the cook sometimes served at dinner, when the butler could not be found. Broderick made his own rules and got away with it.

In Alwyn's opinion, his mother was too indulgent with her servants—another of her many eccentricities. Sometimes that worked to Lord Alwyn's advantage and sometimes it did not.

Returning well after sundown as he had been forced to tonight—there had been important details to go over with Herrick before the morning shift and purchase orders to sign—had evidently thrown the Purcell household into a minor uproar.

Broderick and his underlings, all men fond of drink, were nowhere to be found. He would have to have a little talk with them, in a suitably stern voice, Alwyn decided.

Mrs. Dawkins shrieked at the sight of him and

dropped the tureen, which shattered with an earsplitting crash.

The serving maid clung to the silver basket's handle and glared at him fiercely, as if he intended to take it by force and rob her of the remaining rolls.

Lord Alwyn was hungry enough to do just that. But why were they looking at him as if they saw a ghost?

He whirled around to peer at his reflection in the mirror of the chiffomonster. His hair was no longer black, but stiff and white with mortar dust, and the grime upon his skin had settled into hardened cracks. His green eyes stared wildly back out of his nearly unrecognizable face.

"Mrs. Dawkins, I do apologize." He was very fond of the cook, who had provided forbidden gingerbread and leftover pudding on the sly throughout his childhood. But she ought to have known him. His face had been dirtier than this often enough when he was a lad.

"Hoi! It *is* you, Lord Alwyn! Ye do look a fright!"

"Please do not concern yourself—"

"Beggin' yer pardon, sir, but ye must go in to yer mother before she frets. She does like to see ye at dinner now and then, no matter how ye smell. Did you go a-fishing?"

"Thank you for your kind concern, Mrs. Dawkins," Lord Alwyn said gravely. "Yes, I was fishing, though I had no luck. Old Father Thames gave forth only an old boot."

She nodded, believing his story as she had believed a thousand others over the years, simply out of the goodness of her heart. "Ye'll have better luck when the tide comes in."

The new serving maid edged past, still watching him warily. Mrs. Dawkins bent over to pick up the shards of china and mop up the spilled soup with a napkin, blocking the hallway—his only escape route—with her wide bottom.

He had no choice but to enter the dining room.

Prudence looked up, gave him an enchanting smile—and wrinkled her nose.

Well, if he reeked of fish and worse, there was no help for it. He crossed to the sideboard and poured himself a fortifying and very large glass of brandy, draining the decanter. He drank half before he turned to face the ladies. As he had predicted, his mama was wearing diamond drops in her ears. They looked rather odd with her untidy hair, but he supposed she did not care.

"Good evening, Mama. Good evening, Miss Reese." His mother was chewing assiduously on a difficult piece of chicken and did not answer. Miss Reese only smiled even more enchantingly but she looked as if she wanted to laugh out loud.

Alwyn pulled out a chair and sat, reaching for the platters that Mrs. Dawkins had left, contrary to form, upon the table. He served himself generous portions and devoured what he could before the questions began.

His mother looked at him narrowly, taking several gulps of wine before she spoke.

"My dear boy, what have you done to your hair? Is that some dreadful new fashion? Is Beau Brummell to blame?"

"I hardly think Beau Brummell would powder his hair with dust and mud, Mama. He is a paragon of elegance. Not a cat hair on him."

Lady Agatha raised her eyebrows. "How you talk. Working with bricklayers and carpenters has coarsened you, Alwyn. And you smell very strongly of fish. Did you fall into the river at low tide, perhaps? Becoming a mudlark?" She poked his sleeve to see if it was wet. "No. You are quite dry. Most odd."

"Mama, please do not ask silly questions." He looked to Miss Reese for support, but she was staring into her plate as if new peas in butter sauce were the most fascinating things on earth.

"My dear, I do not see why you have to work so hard, though some—not I—might consider architecture a fit profession for gentlemen. Can you not simply tell that man to finish the building himself?"

"If you mean my master builder, his name is Herrick and he is in charge of a hundred men. As capable as he is, he cannot frame a three-story structure, lay thousands of bricks, and raise a roof on his own." Lord Alwyn finished the rest of his brandy in one go and coughed. He raked a hand through his filthy hair, pulling it up into strange-looking peaks.

"Tell Herrick what it ought to look like, and let him and his men do the rest."

"If only it were that easy." Alywn stretched out his long legs under the table, too exhausted to think of a reply that his mother would accept. His boot—his very muddy boot—touched a slipper-clad foot. Prudence looked up, startled, and pulled her foot away.

Lady Agatha saw fit to change the subject, as the argument was one she knew she would never win. "Do you know, Miss Reese and I have spent a most productive afternoon indoors. Despite the South Seas debacle, my friends have again donated generously. Some of the most erudite works seem not to have been read at all. The young women of London are lucky indeed."

Books—a safe enough subject, Alywn thought. "They must be entertained as well, Mama. Offer stories of undying love to lure them inside the doors. Then you can educate them."

Prudence nodded and he went on, emboldened by her silent approval and the brandy. "Once you have captured one, you can capture them all. Young women flock like geese."

"That is a singularly unflattering comparison, Alwyn," his mother said with a sniff.

He did not heed the warning in that sniff. "You must provide illustrated fairy tales for the younger girls—certainly my small cousins found the stories of Charles Perrault vastly entertaining. I enjoyed reading to them when they were small."

His mother sniffed again. "And now that they are grown, they read nothing but romances."

"But I kept the little darlings out of mischief often enough, did I not? Besides, it was an excellent way to teach them French."

Prudence listened to this exchange with interest. So he liked children and even took the time to read to them. She would not have guessed that, but then she knew very little about him.

Lord Alwyn continued. "And of course, you must have complete sets of Shakespeare's plays—oh, and the sonnets. And poetry—Andrew Marvell's odes, *To His Coy Mistress* and the others—and do not forget Alexander Pope, John Donne, Ben Jonson, and the immortal Chaucer. I shall donate my own volumes of verse, if no one has done so."

Lady Agatha's eyes widened and her mouth turned down in a frown. "Sonnets? Odes to mistresses? The immortal Chaucer is incomprehensible, Alwyn. Next you will be asking me to put frivolous novels and Gothic tales upon the shelves. I shall do no such thing."

"And why not?" he inquired.

His voice was lower than usual and somewhat roughened by liquor and weariness. Prudence found the masculine sound quite thrilling.

"Such things are bad for the female character, which is inherently weaker than that of the male."

He snorted. "I perceive no weakness whatsoever in you, Mama," he began.

"Silence!" she barked. "I will not tolerate such impertinence! And we must not squabble in front of dear Miss Reese! It will impair her digestion!"

The old lady returned her attention to the piece of chicken still on her plate, attacking it ferociously with the wrong fork.

Prudence looked across the table at Lord Alwyn, who gave her a raffish grin.

"Forgive me, Miss Reese, if I have impaired anything of yours. And now, dear ladies, you must excuse me. I am simply too tired to talk tonight and I must wash my hair before this dust sets into stone."

"Ring for the cook."

"She ignores those blasted bells, Mama. You know she does."

Lady Agatha scowled fiercely. "They were installed to remind the sluggish of their duty."

Lord Alwyn leaned back in his chair. "That is the wrong word for her. Mrs. Dawkins is filling in for the lot of them."

"That is as it should be," his mother said peevishly. "Have her send the footman to find your valet."

"I fear the footman has decamped to a dockside tavern with Broderick. They are the best of friends, Mama, and they like to drink each other under the table. It may be a day or two before they return . . . and the whereabouts of my valet are anyone's guess."

Lady Agatha spluttered. "They are more debauched

than your worthless brother! Drinking to excess is a dreadful vice! I fear that Eugene is headed straight to hell."

"Indeed he is, Mama. He seems quite happy about it. Is there any more brandy?"

She waggled her finger at him. "No. I must order more from Dibbles & Hopping. You could send your valet to the pub—"

"Hm. No doubt he is already there. In fact, I am sure he has joined the butler and the footman to sing your praises. You are far too lenient with your male servants and my man has followed their bad example. He disappeared this morning shortly after he shaved me."

He ran a hand over the shadow of beard on his chin, making a faint rasping sound, and looked thoughtfully at Prudence, who blushed.

Lady Agatha harrumphed. "Well, since there is no one else to assist you, *I* shall wash your hair."

Alwyn looked at her, aghast. "Oh, no. You would pull it out by the roots, you are in such a temper. I will manage on my own, Mama."

Prudence wished with all her heart that she could perform this service for him. She looked up longingly as Lord Alwyn rose, bowed to both of them, and left the room.

Chapter Four

Lord Alwyn took the stairs two at a time to the back bedroom that served as his temporary quarters at Purcell House and opened the paneled door.

He shared the room with Marmalady, Mrs. Dawkins's orange cat, terror of the household mice and mother of innumerable kittens of every hue and stripe.

This much-loved and useful animal was permitted to sleep wherever she wished but at the moment she was nowhere to be seen. Her latest offspring could be heard mewing faintly behind the half-open door of the closet.

Marmalady had given birth to them in Alwyn's second-best valise three weeks ago. She seemed to prefer its silk lining and the quiet of the closet to the nest of straw Mrs. Dawkins had prepared for her in the kitchen.

He looked into the valise, where the kittens were lined up in a neat row—a striped one, an orange, two black-and-whites, and a calico—with the head of one upon the back of the next. Ears set low on their round little heads, eyes not yet open, they made a charming picture.

Mrs. Dawkins had approved their new quarters and charged Alwyn with their care. No one was permitted to move the little family without permission from Marmalady or her, the cook had explained dramatically.

He looked around, hoping that the vanished valet had at least left him clean water in the ewer—ah, Joseph had. Very good. And the matching basin held water as well.

He kicked the door shut, in too much of a hurry to notice that it had not closed all the way.

Alwyn quickly took off his reeking coat and looked about for a place to put it. The deep outer windowsill held a large, empty flowerbox—it would have to do.

Stuffing the coat into it, he remained standing to pull off his boots—no easy task—to prevent the upholstered chair from absorbing the unmistakable odor of haddock upon his clothes.

As for the muddy boots, he could not simply drop them upon the costly Turkey carpet. His man would have to brush and polish them for the morrow—if Joseph ever returned from carousing.

Lord Alwyn put the boots into the closet atop a box of rags, taking care not to disturb the slumbering heap of kittens in the valise.

His linen shirt and buckskins followed the coat into the flowerbox, but he left his flannel drawers on. These he wore for comfort, as the construction site was often cold. It had been even colder than usual tonight and the brandy he'd drunk had not warmed him sufficiently to consider complete nakedness at the moment.

He took a deep breath and braced himself to soak his hair in the basin of cold water. More than anything, he hated cold water. It made him gasp and it chilled him to the bone. Only a deep, deep featherbed and a lusty lass to hold through the night could warm him now.

He imagined holding Miss Prudence Reese in just such a featherbed and felt positively hot all over. Of course, his mama would lecture him severely if he compromised Prudence's reputation in the slightest, but a man could dream, could he not?

He grinned at his reflection in the mirror above the basin. Below the neck, his skin was perfectly clean, but above it—he did look a fright, as Mrs. Dawkins had said. Alwyn wondered how Prudence had kept from laughing at the dinner table.

She had evidently not told Mama about his adventure in the revolving basket, for the old lady had not mentioned it. And Prudence had displayed admirable composure, despite his mother's scathing comments and the petty squabble that had followed.

The more he thought about her, the more it seemed that he—*No*, he told himself sternly. An honorable man did not carry on frivolous flirtations with females living under the same roof. And he was in no position to marry, as his work consumed nearly all of his time.

He had no fortune, he reminded himself. The thought was depressing in the extreme.

He scrubbed his face vigorously with a wet washcloth, straightened up, and gave the mirror a big, bold smile. Chin up. That was the ticket. Life held infinite possibilities.

Once the Purcell Library for Women was built, there would be grander commissions to come. He hoped to go down in history as an architect to rival the immortal Inigo Jones or even England's most celebrated genius, Sir Christopher Wren.

Alwyn looked at his reflection again, almost

alarmed at the sight of his strangely spiky hair. He would go down in history as a circus ape dancing on a chain if he did not plunge in now, cold water or no.

He bent over the basin once more, and picked up his shaving cup to sluice the water over his head. It trickled over his scalp, raising goosebumps that were almost painful, and into his ears.

Alwyn wanted to howl but he continued to dip the cup and wet his hair, unaware that Marmalady had sidled into the room, pushing open the door.

He fumbled, eyes half-shut, for the cake of Spanish soap, remembering too late that he had not set any by the basin. Damnation!

He would have to go downstairs and beg some from Mrs. Dawkins. The slippery concoction of lye and grease that she used for washing-up would probably dissolve his hair.

He straightened to look about for a towel, which, in his haste, he had also neglected to set by the basin.

Rivulets of cold water trickled down his back. Alwyn shivered. The water reached his flannel drawers and soaked them *and* his bum. Was there no end to this misery? And how had the blasted cat, suddenly twining herself about his ankles like a vine, got in?

"Oh! Pray excuse me!"

He looked up into Prudence's beautiful blue eyes.

Chapter Five

"You have a rare talent for appearing in unexpected places, Miss Reese!"

Prudence was momentarily at a loss for a suitable reply. Instead, she took in the glorious sight of Lord Alwyn nearly naked: his broad chest and the fine dark hair upon it, his smooth-skinned, strong shoulders, and his muscular middle.

The cold water dripping down his body only heightened his masculine beauty, which was very like that of a Greek statue, she thought, marveling silently. If Greek statues wore flannel drawers that laced at the waist. She looked away.

"I suppose you will say that the cat opened the door." He glared at her, hands on his narrow hips, not even trying to cover himself up.

"I did not. Your door was ajar and I had no idea that you were bathing."

The cat yowled for attention and rubbed against Lord Alwyn's shins, provoking him further. "Do shut up. See to your kittens, old thing." Marmalady gave him an accusing, yellow-eyed glare and he realized he had turned the closet latch when he put his boots inside. "Oh—you are unable to enter. Forgive me, my dear Mrs. Marmalady."

He reached out a long arm and turned the latch the other way, staying rooted to the spot.

"I only wanted to return something to you," Prudence said in a slightly dazed voice.

"Well, what is it?" he asked brusquely. Having caught him nearly naked, why did she not run away? He was embarrassed beyond measure, but unable to do aught but stand there, lest he reveal more.

Prudence gaped at him, evidently forgetting what it was she had intended to return. She held a small book that looked somewhat familiar. Perhaps that was it. Knowing that she had come upstairs to see him on so slight a pretext pleased him.

"Ahem—please forgive my impatience, Miss Reese. But I must dress and you must leave."

She kept her eyes firmly fixed on his face, no doubt trying to avoid looking lower. The intensity of her gaze was unnerving.

Alwyn stood stock-still. Turning around to find a robe, a blanket, anything, would mean showing his soaked drawers, which were clinging to his bum.

That sight might very well shatter her composure, though of course his bum was not in any way remarkable—it was a very ordinary bum, assuredly, like thousands of other bums. Alwyn sighed. He was losing his wits, he was certain of it.

At that moment, there was a familiar wheeze at the bottom of the stairs, and his mother's imperious voice called up.

"Proooo-dence! Are you retiring for the night? I should not have napped. I will never sleep. Shall we play cards?"

"Yes! Oh yes!" Her heart leapt with joy. She would seize any chance to escape her predicament, would even allow the old lady to win. "I shall be down presently."

That answer seemed to satisfy Lady Agatha, who moved away, humming an odd little song.

Prudence searched Lord Alwyn's expression for a clue to his thoughts, but he simply stared at her, though not quite so fiercely.

"Miss Reese, you said you had something to return to me. Is that it?" He nodded at the small book she clutched with white-knuckled fingers. She looked at it as if she had no idea how it had come to be in her hands.

"Yes . . . the *Moral Discourses* of Bishop Applegate."

Lord Alwyn rolled his eyes and crossed his arms over his chest. "Ah. No doubt you think my soul needs saving."

His arrogant tone piqued her. "That is none of my affair, sir. But when we met this morning, you did mention drawings." She hesitated.

What had that to do with Bishop Applegate's book? "I found the drawings I was looking for, thank you."

"Oh. Then perhaps this—these are not yours."

"You are talking in riddles, Miss Reese. What is not mine?"

"This book. I shall keep it." She held it over her heart.

Lord Alwyn shrugged. Then he shivered. His soaked drawers were damned uncomfortable and he was chilled to the bone. "As you wish. I had not known that you were so religious, but come to think of it, I should thank you for praying for me whilst I was suspended between heaven and earth."

"What?" she asked.

"I could not thank you at dinner, you understand.

In any case, it seemed that God was listening, as I landed safely."

Should she contradict him? She had clasped her hands not to pray but to catch a moth, so that it would not fly through the window and wake the slumbering Lady Agatha.

Perhaps he fancied himself a great hero for having been hoisted to the heavens in a basket, but she had not worried about him for one second.

"Good-night, Miss Reese."

"What?" she asked again.

He smiled at last—rather gently, she thought, surprised.

"I said good-night. Much as I am enjoying this impromptu conversation, I cannot continue it dressed—or rather undressed—as I am. You do understand."

She nodded. "Oh, quite."

"The book is mine, however. Look inside the flyleaf. Applegate signed it. 'To Lord Alwyn Purcell, with my gracious compliments unto eternity,' or some such nonsense."

Prudence opened the book ever so carefully, so the small drawings would not fall out once more, and looked at the dedication. He was right.

"But you may keep it," he said suddenly. "I have not read it and I am not likely to."

She looked at the book and at him. Did the delicately sensual artwork within belong to him? She found it impossible to ask.

A dull game of cards with Lady Agatha was just the thing to settle her agitated nerves, Prudence thought, stifling a yawn. They had been at it for over an hour.

The quiet slap of the playing cards upon the green baize-covered table, her companion's tedious humming, and the effort to remember the simple rules gave her something to think about besides Lord Alwyn.

In only one day, she had discovered much about him: his admirable passion for his work, his romantic taste in literature, his intelligence, his *joie de vivre*—and his amorous nature.

She also knew what he looked like in the humblest of garments: plain flannel drawers. He looked . . . magnificent. Prudence was wildly attracted to him, but knew instinctively that Lady Agatha would not approve.

Nor would her own mother. Lady Felicia thought that younger sons were an utter waste of time, although she had married one and borne several children by him. But once she had washed her hands of their papa, she advised all her daughters not to do as she had done.

Therefore, Prudence thought, she would not indulge in moony dreams of love with the rakish Lord Alwyn. Such a fantasy was no more real than the amorous rendezvous depicted in the lovely drawings she had found.

To hide them from prying eyes, she had gone to her own chamber after her encounter with Lord Alwyn, concealing both the drawings and the book hastily beneath her neatly folded chemises in the wardrobe.

Prudence wondered if the drawings were valuable. Of course, she would not sell them, though her most pressing concerns were financial. Despite having been taught only a dash of arithmetic, she kept careful track of her money and permitted herself not the smallest extravagance. The allowance that her mama had pressed into her hand upon her leavetaking was nearly gone.

Unlike that lady, who thought but lightly of borrowing from her relations and never thought of repaying these loans at all, Prudence hated to owe. But, gently bred as she was, there seemed to be no respectable way for her to earn a living, however much a desire to do so burned within her.

No matter which way she looked at it, she was dependent to a very great degree upon the kindness of her extended family.

While supervising the packing of Prudence's few gowns for her first London season, Prudence's mama had reminded her bluntly that marriage was the only way out. She'd added that Prudence was tolerably pretty, if penniless, and that any daughter of hers ought to be able to bag a rich husband.

For that reason and others she would not name, she had been happy to commend Prudence to the care of Lady Agatha. In some ways, Prudence reflected, the old lady had been very like a mother to her. It was an interesting sensation.

Lady Agatha was generous to a fault. And Lady Felicia, having squandered all of her income and even attacked her principal to pay for her own gowns and jewelry over the years, had somehow persuaded Agatha to cover the costs of her youngest daughter's debut—an occasion that Prudence dreaded.

Her older sisters had already come out *and* married, and she was the last fledgling to venture timidly from the downy confines of the parental nest. No, she thought, smiling to herself as she studied her cards. Her dear mama had simply tossed her out to see whether she could fly.

Prudence's father, an inconsequential third son of a long-lived earl, had gone abroad years ago to make his fortune with the East India Company and never returned. It was said that he had become a dealer in gemstones and pearls, then acquired a harem and lost track of the number of his subsequent children. These interesting reports could not be confirmed, however.

Prudence was to make her debut all the same. But nothing had been bought thus far, and there seemed to be no end to what she might need.

Simply choosing the right finery in which to be presented to her sovereign was a daunting task. Whenever Agatha could spare an afternoon from fretting over the library, they had made the rounds of the shops and modistes together, and come up empty-handed.

Prudence had politely said no to every gown her old relation liked, and vice versa. They were no closer to deciding than they had been several weeks ago, and the date for the traditional ceremony at the Court of St. James was drawing near.

Of course, Prudence would be the cynosure of all eyes no matter what she wore—and the subject of critical whispers for the brief time it took to be announced, curtsy, and walk backwards out of the royal presence.

What if her feathers stood crookedly in her hair? What if she stepped on someone else's train and fell flat on her face? She did not even want to think about it.

Lady Agatha muttered something and squinted

rather crossly at the cards in her hands, as though she saw no chance of winning.

Prudence settled deeper into her chair, thinking over her situation. At least she felt quite welcome at Purcell House, though keeping up with the odd fancies and enthusiasms of her benefactress was tiring at times. If nothing else, cataloguing the books that filled the uppermost story provided a temporary distraction.

But she could not avoid preparing for her debut forever. To delay it much longer might bring her mother to London.

Prudence set down her cards with a sigh, bracing herself to bring up the subject, but Lady Agatha continued to hum, oblivious to everything but her losing hand.

Suddenly, a flash of orange fur at the tall window in back of the old lady caught Prudence's eye. Was that Marmalady?

It was. The old cat held a kitten—the striped one—tenderly in her mouth as she picked her way over the roof tiles and disappeared from view. She returned without it in a minute or two.

Then a much larger creature on all fours came creeping along the edge of the roof. Prudence simply stared. It was Lord Alwyn, still wearing his flannel drawers, but now with a loose-fitting shirt, clean but somewhat tattered, tucked into them.

He put a finger to his lips to tell her to be silent. Wide-eyed, Prudence obeyed. She prayed that Lady Agatha would not turn around.

Chapter Six

Why was Marmalady moving her kittens? And was Lord Alwyn assisting her in some way—or was he simply a lunatic who roamed the roof at night for his own amusement? No one had seen fit to warn her of this.

Lady Agatha ceased her humming and pulled her shawl more tightly around her shoulders, frowning at her cards once more.

Prudence jumped up. "There is a draft!" She scurried to the window and fussed with the velvet drapery, looking out at Lord Alwyn, whose face was only inches away. He said something inaudible. She studied his sensual lips as he repeated it slowly.

Do . . . not . . . talk. He pointed to his mother's shawl-draped back.

Prudence nodded.

He pointed at the cat, which sidled away. *If . . . Marmalady . . . falls . . .*

She nodded again and waited anxiously.

He held an imaginary gun to his head.

Mrs . . . Dawkins . . . will . . . shoot . . . me.

"Oh, dear!"

Lady Agatha did not bother to turn around. "Whatever is the matter, Prudence? Is there something you need? Ring for the butler—no, ring for Mrs. Dawkins."

Through the window, Prudence saw Lord Alwyn shake his head wildly. "I am sure she is asleep, Lady Agatha. Exciting as our game has been, I myself am somewhat drowsy. And you?" Prudence jerked the draperies closed and left Lord Alwyn to his own devices for the moment.

Ever in need of a nap, the stout old lady nodded. And yawned. "A trifle."

"Dear Lady Agatha, allow me to entertain you at the pianoforte. Perhaps some gentle airs—or lullabies?"

Lady Agatha yawned again, peering blearily at her cards. She positively creaked as she turned around to look at her young relation. "You are very thoughtful, Prudence. Please play whatever you wish."

Prudence looked through the music. Military marches—no. Scottish jigs—no. Exuberant reels and sprightly country dances—no, no, no. She found a single sheet covered with repeating chords. It looked like a monotonous composition exercise scribbled by a child. Precisely the thing. She began to play, very softly.

"I shall declare myself the winner of this round, if you don't mind," Lady Agatha said. "And perhaps I shall lie down. That is a very pretty melody, Prudence. It scarcely seems to change, but that is all to the good."

The old lady rose with some difficulty and headed for the divan. She settled in, folding her hands and tucking them under her cheek, and was asleep in less than a minute.

Prudence played on for a little while longer, then tiptoed to the window, looking around this way and that to see . . . nothing at all. The roof was empty, illuminated by the moon above. There was no sign

of Lord Alwyn—or the cat that had brought him
out upon the roof.

He was not far away, though he was not in sight.
Alwyn observed Marmalady step through an opening cut for a dormer room that was covered with
canvas because there was no window as yet. Her kitten swung perilously in her mouth as she slipped
behind the canvas and out of sight.

He would have to catch her, and bring the kitten
down. The unfinished dormer was not safe.

But Marmalady would not take kindly to a
change in her plans, and she tended not to listen to
men, though she seemed to like him well enough.
She left orange fur on most of his clothing, Alwyn
thought ruefully.

Perhaps Miss Reese could make the cat listen to
reason. Her soft voice was undoubtedly quite per-
suasive.

The canvas flapped and Marmalady came out.
Thus far she had moved only one kitten, but she
was sure to move the others—and soon. He considered pouncing upon her but she sat upon the
roof, just out of reach, and gave him a baleful look.

Alwyn deeply regretted placing his fishy-smelling,
muddy boots next to her nursery, obviously a most
unhygienic arrangement in Marmalady's motherly
opinion.

There was no use arguing with a cat, he knew.

He made a move toward her, looking sideways, in
the vain hope that the cat would think he was not
interested in her. Marmalady did not seem fooled.
She sidled away.

Alwyn sat. For a minute or two, he admired the

half-built walls of his mother's library two lots over, glad to be able to study the construction without the dizzying distraction of the basket. Perhaps Charles was right. The walls did seem ever so slightly out of plumb, but he would have to measure to be sure.

Tomorrow morning, first thing, he would bring his instruments and perform the necessary calculations. Tonight he had a cat to catch.

He slid one bare leg over the tiles, searching for a foothold above the window where he had glimpsed Miss Reese and Lady Agatha at cards—and felt his ankle firmly grasped by a feminine hand.

"Lord Alwyn!" Her voice was an emphatic whisper. "You will break your neck if you are not careful! Whatever are you doing?"

There was no use arguing with Prudence either. Not in so precarious a position, with one leg up and one leg down, and barefoot. He sighed and regained his balance. "Will you help me, Miss Reese? I must catch the cat and get her kitten to safety. She might come if you call her."

Prudence craned her neck to look up at him but she kept a firm grip on his ankle. The sensation of her soft hand holding on so tightly was most unsettling. He breathed a sigh of relief when she let go.

"How am I to get up there?"

She clasped the windowsill and gave him an anxious look.

"Climb out. Mama is asleep, is she not?"

Prudence looked back into the room and nodded. "She is. Excuse me for a moment while I see to her comfort."

He sat back, crossed one leg over the other and tapped a foot nonchalantly, as if he were in a nice, safe drawing room and not prowling in his unmentionables amidst the chimneypots because of a wretched cat.

For all he knew, Marmalady would sit there forever. Or perhaps not. Her kittens would soon be hungry and their tiny mews always brought her running. Perhaps the thing to do was find the one in the dormer and use it to lure her closer.

A slight breeze ruffled Marmalady's fur and his own damp hair. Should he tell Miss Reese to bring a shawl? No—it might impair her ability to climb. Worse, it might cover up her admirably lissome body.

Fortunately for him, the dark slate tiles still held the warmth of the day's strong sun and he was not cold, even half-dressed as he was.

That would be reason enough for her to refuse his most improper invitation. Not only that, but if anyone saw them—well, if anyone saw them he could explain, he supposed.

Still, his situation was most undignified. In a well-run household, the pursuit of cats would be left to the nimbler servants. But, as he had suspected, his mother's men were happily carousing at the nearby tavern. The pageboy, whom Alwyn had roused from sleep on his way up here, had confirmed it.

Should a friend or acquaintance happen by and see him and Miss Reese upon the roof, he would say that they were studying the lunar seas. The nearly full moon was bright enough.

Lady Agatha's snoring could be clearly heard through the open window as Prudence popped her head out. "She might wake," Prudence whispered. "I cannot be sure."

Lord Alwyn shrugged. "That is a chance you will have to take. But I doubt it. My dear mother can sleep anywhere, at any time. Every sofa in the house bears her imprint."

"I had noticed that."

With a mixture of surprise and delight, Alwyn watched Prudence pull up her skirts as modestly as she was able, and extend a foot, clad in a blue-and-white striped slipper, outwards. She braced herself with her hands and straddled the sill.

It was flat and wide. Prudence would be safe enough. He was glad indeed that he had insisted upon a restrained design for this house and pooh-poohed his dear mama's proposal for an Indian-inspired fantasy, bristling with minarets and decorative domes and oriental ornament.

Brighton was the place for such eccentric architecture, its painted palms and exotic hodgepodge all very well for a grand dinner or a ball, but not a respectable family's house.

Aha! Lord Alwyn was delighted to see Prudence's light dress slide up and reveal lace-trimmed pantaloons as she wriggled out, holding on to the window frame but not tightly. Clearly she had been the sort of girl who climbed trees and played the hoyden.

But she could not be expected to climb up to where he was entirely on her own. It was time for him to play the gallant and come to her rescue.

"Wait!" he hissed dramatically. "You will break *your* neck! Allow me to assist you!"

She smiled dazzlingly at him. Had she been clad only in moonlight, she could not have been more beautiful at that moment, poised on the edge as if eager to be swept up in his arms.

The ledge on which she perched was too narrow for that degree of gallantry, he thought nervously.

He edged closer and extended a hand to aid her. "Do be careful, my dear Miss Reese. And welcome to the roof."

She slipped her hand into his and stepped toward him as gracefully as a dancer, seeming unperturbed by the height—and employing a tree-climber's trick of not looking down, he noted approvingly.

"Thank you, Lord Alwyn. It is a pleasure to be here. The night is very fine." She looked around, enjoying the moonlit view of London and the gentle breeze. The view of Alwyn's manly chest—there were a few holes in his worn linen shirt—was even better, in her opinion.

Prudence made a mental note of it, should she happen to write a romance after all. Though she had given the idea little thought since leafing through *The Persuasion of Pamela Jones* and had no plot and no particular setting in mind, a clandestine rooftop meeting with a handsome man in a tattered shirt seemed like an excellent way to begin any love story.

His voice interrupted her literary musing.

"Indeed it is," he said. "Very fine indeed."

Could he not come up with something more intelligent to say, he thought, chagrined. He had never made small talk wearing small clothes—well, perhaps he had. But never with so charming and innocent a companion, nor in such compromising circumstances.

Of course, he would not breathe a word of this to anyone and he doubted she would. Miss Prudence Reese was not the type to gossip, he suspected. He realized that he was still holding her hand. Should he let go? He did not want to—and she did not withdraw it.

She looked over towards the library. She could just see the half-built walls from this height. "I should like to ride in the basket and go round and round, as you did."

Even the memory made him queasy. "It is not an experience that a lady would enjoy, Miss Reese."

"I am sure that I would," she said decisively.

Marmalady greeted her with a meow, watching them both through narrowed eyes.

"Hm," he said to the cat, "what are we going to do about you?"

Marmalady yawned in a rude way.

Alwyn's next words were for Prudence. "If we can retrieve her kitten from that room"—he gestured toward the unfinished dormer—"she will follow us readily enough."

Prudence nodded. "And am I to get the kitten?"

"You will fit more easily through that opening than I," Alwyn pointed out.

"Very well." She let go of his hand and proceeded to the dormer without further ado. As he watched, delighted by her boldness, she lifted up the canvas, peering inside and listening with her head tipped to one side.

The evening breeze carried the sound of a faint mew.

"Ah—I hear it." Prudence kneeled and crept in on all fours as Alwyn kept an eye on Marmalady. It was no more than a minute before she came out, cradling the tiny kitten in one hand.

The mother cat mewed anxiously, rubbing against Alwyn's ankles as Prudence came closer to give him the kitten.

Before he put it down his shirt, which had miraculously remained tucked into the snug waistband of his drawers, he let the kitten rest in his cupped hand, and held it against his heart for a moment.

He was rewarded with an approving smile from Prudence, who stroked the kitten's head with a fingertip, looking at it tenderly. She stood rather too close and he felt an unmistakable stirring in his loins.

Oh, no. Oh, God. His body would betray him if his eyes did not. He looked away from her and thought of other things. Cold water. *Very* cold water. That did the trick.

The kitten nestled happily in Alwyn's chest hair but he grimaced when its tiny claws pricked his skin. "Ow! You will have to behave better than that, my small friend."

It retracted its claws and began to knead rhythmically upon the thickest hair in the center of his chest, emitting an infinitesimal purr.

"Your guest seems to like its lodgings," Prudence said impishly. "It wants only milk to be perfectly happy."

Lord Alwyn raised an eyebrow in amusement. "There is a limit to what a man can do." He took the kitten from his chest and settled it lower, using his tucked-in shirt as a bag of sorts.

Prudence giggled but Marmalady seemed to find nothing at all funny about the situation. The cat batted at Alwyn's bare legs with one paw but he ignored her, reaching out to Prudence once more to guide her back to the window. "Shall we, Miss Reese?"

She clasped his hand again and Alwyn congratulated himself on his derring-do. Rescuing a small animal was an excellent way to impress a woman, evidently. He would have to keep that in mind.

There came a shout. "Hoi!" And another. "I say!" And another. "Damme, if it ain't himself and our Miss Prudence, up on the roof like a couple of thieves in the night!"

The footman and the butler—and worst of all, his valet—were staring up at them from the street below, mouths agape and bleary eyes wide.

"Quiet!" thundered Lord Alwyn—and then he remembered his mother. Would she wake? An awful silence fell over the street. The three servants looked at each other as if they did not know what to say or do next.

Prudence tugged at his hand. The sooner they were back inside, the better for all concerned. She hoped not to attract a crowd and speed was of the essence. As the men looked on, they went in through the window, Prudence first, Lord Alwyn second, and Marmalady last.

Once they were all safely upon the carpet, Prudence waved to the threesome on the street below and tossed them what she hoped was an innocent smile, then shut the window and drew the curtain.

There would have to be explanations, but she would leave that to himself, to use the valet's term.

The kitten shifted within the shirt and Marmalady pricked up her ears at the sound of its mewling.

"Hurry!" Prudence whispered. "We can bring this one and the rest into my room. But we cannot linger here!" She pointed to the slumbering figure of his mother, grateful that the old lady's eyes were still closed, her breathing deep and regular. Her snoring had stopped.

As they tiptoed past, neither noticed Lady

Agatha's left eye open ever so slightly—and shut tight once more.

Prudence and Alwyn entered the upstairs hall and bumped into the red-haired maid who had helped serve the dinner.

"Oh, Cathy, perhaps you can help us," Prudence said, happy to see her.

"Please do not stare," Lord Alwyn said, assuming a dignified air that did not quite make up for his lack of proper clothing. "Drawers are not so very different from breeches."

The maid glanced down inadvertently at his drawers and then up again. "Yes, sir." Marmalady, at his ankles once more, made a soft inquiry and the small lump at Alwyn's waist responded. "Your shirt, sir—it is mewing."

"Yes, I know. We have rescued one of Marmalady's kittens and we must move the others before she brings them all to the roof. Miss Reese has kindly volunteered the use of her room."

Prudence nodded. "If you will help us carry the others, we would be very much obliged."

"Certainly, miss." Cathy smiled, seeming pleased to be entrusted with the task.

They proceeded up the flight of stairs to the bedroom in question and looked about for a place to put the kitten, who was now climbing up Alwyn's bare flesh with a determination most remarkable for so small a being.

He looked down to note its progress inside his shirt and winced. "The little devil is pricking me unmercifully."

"Hm. And I thought you strong, Lord Alwyn—and

brave enough to wrestle tigers and lions," Prudence teased.

He cast her a quizzical look. "You have no reason to think any such thing. We scarcely know each other." He plucked the striped kitten from his chest and held it out to her. "You may wrestle this tiger if you like."

Marmalady was nearly frantic with worry, and Cathy bent down to pet her. "There, there. Ye'll have it back soon enough. Miss Reese, should we move their bed to the wardrobe? There is room enough."

"An excellent suggestion," Alwyn said.

The maid straightened and opened the wardrobe's door, taking a few seconds to tidy the pile of folded chemises. And then . . .

Damnation! Prudence nearly swore aloud. Out tumbled the bishop's book and, from its pages, the hidden drawings of the amorous encounter in the garden.

"Oh!" she exclaimed, turning scarlet. "*Moral Discourses*! However did that get there?" She handed the kitten to Cathy, much to Marmalady's annoyance.

One glance at the drawings and Alwyn understood. Too swiftly for the maid to see their subject, he bent down to pick them up. "Are these yours, Miss Reese?" He looked at them closely.

"Indeed not," she said indignantly.

"Well, then I shall keep them," he said brazenly, and slipped the drawings inside his shirt. "And you may keep Bishop Applegate's *Discourses* to read at your leisure."

Enfolding the kitten carefully within her apron,

Cathy picked up the book and set it aside. "Shall I fetch the others, sir?"

Alwyn nodded. "Yes. They are in an old valise at the bottom of my closet. Miss Reese and I will prepare a bed."

The maid dropped a curtsy and left. Prudence and Alwyn simply stood there for a moment, looking at each other.

"The drawings . . ." she began. "I am sorry." She stopped, feeling very awkward. To explain why she had hidden them—or how she had found them in the first place—was simply impossible.

"I assure you, there is no need to apologize," Lord Alwyn said with a twinkle. "An interest in art is a very good thing in a female."

"Art. Yes." Her tongue seemed to be tied in a knot of embarrassment. To be so close twice in one day to an exceedingly handsome, half-dressed man was a trial indeed. To have naughty pictures found amidst her intimate attire was even worse.

"Though the book is mine, as I said, I have no idea how those drawings came to be inside it. Do you, Miss Reese?"

Prudence shook her head wildly. "No. None whatsoever."

He withdrew one from his shirt and looked at it again. "It is original work—and finely drawn—but not signed. Where are the others?"

"What do you mean?"

He held the drawing out to her. "This mark indicates that it is one of fifteen. But you have only five."

"I have not the slightest idea if there are others or where they might be."

Whatever was keeping Cathy? Prudence could not simply stay here and chat about such things.

She wondered suddenly if Alwyn had put the drawings inside the book—it seemed just the sort of thing he might do. Though how could he predict that she would ultimately find them? Perhaps he had hidden them there some time ago.

Prudence did not want to admit that she had kicked the little book under the desk to keep his mama from reading it aloud—or that she had tried to throw it away—and then kept it once she found the drawings.

He slipped the one in his hand back inside his shirt with the others and looked at her again. There was no mistaking the significance of the gleam in his eye, she thought nervously.

But his tone was polite when he finally spoke. "You are full of surprises, Miss Reese."

She took a step back and glared at him. "You cannot presume that I had anything to do with—oh, I suspect this is all your mischief!" she burst out. "Do you remember? I asked you before about them, when I was in—just outside, I mean—your room. You said only this morning that you had mislaid some drawings."

"My dear lady, I meant architectural drawings—not these seductive sketches. In any case, I would rather look at a real woman than one on paper."

He seemed upon the verge of laughter and his fine mouth quirked at one corner. Mortified, Prudence took another step back. What if he were to seize the opportunity to kiss her again? If the maid returned and saw them, she would be in a perfect pickle.

She heard footsteps approach and breathed a

sigh of relief. But the person who came into the room was not Cathy. Lady Agatha had awakened at last.

Chapter Seven

"My dear, I do apologize for dozing off. I was so surprised to find that you had gone when I woke up!"

"Yes. I decided to retire earlier than usual."

Was that an adequate explanation? Prudence could not be sure. Considering how prudish Lady Agatha sometimes was, it was odd that the old lady did not remark upon the presence of Alwyn in her bedroom. In his drawers. She seemed not to notice her son's state of undress at all.

Prudence wondered why.

"I met Cathy upon the stairs. She said that you are moving the kittens. Is this wise, Alwyn? You know how Mrs. Dawkins feels about that cat."

"It was Marmalady who took it upon herself to do so, Mama, not I. She brought one to the roof. Miss Reese assisted in its rescue."

She bestowed a nod of approval upon Prudence. "You are intrepid, my dear."

Alwyn and Prudence exchanged a look. Did Lady Agatha know that they had been up on the roof, alone in the moonlight? As if they could read each other's minds, they made a silent mutual vow to say nothing of it.

Cathy bustled back in, her apron now full of

squirming kittens, followed by Marmalady, meowing loudly. Prudence sprang toward the wardrobe and hastily lined a basket resting on the lowest shelf with an old housedress.

Cathy knelt to put them inside one by one, detaching their delicate claws from the fabric of her apron with great care. Marmalady jumped in without further ado. She curled around them, pinning each with a paw for a rough-and-ready bath before she would allow it to nurse.

"She is an excellent mother," Lady Agatha said softly. "Though it is a thankless task often enough. How soon children grow up!" She wiped away a very small tear.

"My dear Mama," said Alwyn with astonishment. "I have never known you to be sentimental on that subject."

Lady Agatha drew herself up and gave him an imperious look. "Do you think I have no heart?"

"No, no—not at all," he hastened to assure her. "Of course you have a heart. A very kind heart . . ." She waved away his praise, but he could see she was pleased.

When Lady Agatha busied herself with the basket, assisted by Cathy, Alwyn winked at Prudence, who did a most unexpected thing. She winked back.

Devil take it! Was this sweet young thing flirting with him? She was bold indeed—but how extraordinarily delicious! He had half a mind to let himself into her chamber later tonight, and steal another kiss. Nothing more. Clearly she was attracted to him. He gave her a self-satisfied smile.

As if reading his mind, Lady Agatha straightened up with one hand upon the wardrobe and the other upon the maid's shoulder and fixed him with a basilisk stare.

For the first time, she seemed to notice Alwyn's attire—or lack of it—and scowled fiercely at him. "Hm. Your drawers need washing and that shirt is fit only for the ragbag. It is full of holes. And why have you put paper inside it?"

He put a hand over the drawings. "Ah—to keep me warm."

"Tut-tut. You need a woman's care, Alwyn. My son should not stuff papers in his shirt and run about in dirty drawers."

Prudence turned away to hide her amusement. Perhaps she should not have winked, for he had looked insufferably pleased with himself from that moment on. She was happy to see that Lady Agatha had taken him down a peg. No one could do it better than a mother.

For his part, Alwyn felt more than a little chagrined. Even Cathy was staring straight ahead, her lips compressed. No doubt the maid was amused by his predicament as well. "They were clean when I put them on, Mama, though somewhat damp."

"And why was that?" Lady Agatha inquired. "Are you not amply provided with dry drawers, as befits a young man of fashion?"

Was the shadow of a smile lurking about his mother's stern mouth? He could not be sure.

He cleared his throat. "There was no towel by my bath. And I was interrupted by—the cat." He glared at Prudence, who ignored him.

"Surely Marmalady did not prevent you from putting on proper clothes, Alwyn."

"Mama! I was about to retire for the night when

I went out after that damned cat—and I prefer to sleep in old linen."

Lady Agatha sniffed. "Do not swear. It is dirty linen now. You must change or your sheets will be black as coal." She waved at him. "Go."

He bowed ever so slightly and withdrew from Prudence's bedroom, turned on his heel in the hall, and walked away with all the dignity he could summon. A gentleman carried himself with pride, no matter what.

The sound of a muffled snort reached his ears and he cringed inwardly at the sound of the three women smothering their laughter as he walked away. He made an ineffectual attempt to brush the soot from his backside. So much for his pride.

He would not sleep well, he knew. He did not regret his brief interlude in the charming company of Miss Reese, of course. But he had made a fool of himself without quite knowing how.

No, he reflected sourly. His dear mama had made a fool of him, of that he was sure.

The sun was high in the sky when the household staff bestirred itself the next day.

The first to awake, Lord Alwyn requested a proper breakfast from the estimable Mrs. Dawkins and Cathy. The cook made so bold as to inquire about the state of his drawers before she gave him a broad wink and left with the serving maid. Evidently Cathy had told her everything.

Feeling very much out of sorts, he rang for the butler, the footman, and his valet, and lectured them for a quarter of an hour on their conduct last night. Standing in a row, the servants assumed un-

convincing expressions of regret throughout his
tirade, perhaps because he was forced to keep
his voice low and to offer a small remuneration
in return for their silence on the subject of what
they saw.

His dear mama and Miss Reese sauntered into the
breakfast room somewhat later. Their morning
robes seemed to clash with the bright yellow flowers
of the wallpaper, which had never gone with the
striped chairs anyway. Unable to control his irritation, he vowed to say nothing for as long as possible.

His mother might object to his silence or she
might not. She was a bit scatterbrained at the best of
times, of course, and there was no predicting what
she might say or do. He sometimes suspected her of
being considerably more clever than she let on.

The ensuing meal was mostly silent, save for the
crunch of toast and the rustle of turning pages as
Lord Alwyn read a large architectural treatise.

Prudence looked round the coffee pot to read its
title. He seemed disinclined to talk or to show his
face.

"*The Principles and Practice of Classical Architecture.*
That sounds most interesting," she said brightly.

He said nothing.

His mother, clad in a silk robe and matching turban and sitting at a small table by the window,
sipped her tea with obvious enjoyment. "Reverend
Ponsonby said we should count our blessings before breakfast. I myself have too many to count.
And you, Alwyn?" Her wrinkled, intelligent face
turned to the morning sun.

Lady Agatha looked as contented as a turtle upon
a warm rock, Prudence thought. The same could
not be said for Lord Alwyn, who ignored his

mother's question but lowered the treatise to look at Prudence for a moment.

To her surprise, he mumbled something that resembled a "good morning," and ran a hand through his hair, which was uncombed though certainly dashing in its messy way, in Prudence's opinion. She would not mind running her own hands through it.

Duty done, Lord Alwyn hid behind the treatise again. He wanted to howl with frustration. How could Miss Reese look so utterly beguiling at such an early hour? Her tumbling curls and sleepy blush would tempt the devil himself. He told himself to think of other things and stared fixedly at the page in front of him.

He reminded himself that he was a man of reason, a man of culture. Classical architecture ought to be just as beguiling as a mere female in artless deshabille. For as long as possible, he studied a chart of the mathematical ratios that the ancient Greeks used to produce architectural harmony.

Unfortunately, Miss Reese's harmonious ratios were all too evident in that soft morning robe, which clung to her slender form. He swore under his breath, and turned the page.

The next chapter began with an etching of a ruined temple. He studied this carefully for several minutes. It was a magnificent structure, even if most of the façade had been destroyed. Yet one thick column remained, thrusting proudly skyward. Gracing the temple roof were twin domes, rounder than a woman's—

It was no use. He turned to the back page and stared at the index until the fine print grew blurry. He wasn't safe within fifty miles of Miss Reese.

Prudence knew nothing of the struggle that was

going on within his soul. She played idly with the jam spoon and looked about.

Out of the corner of her eye she saw Marmalady enter and head straight for Lord Alwyn. Surely the attentions of the animal would annoy him, Prudence thought.

Without taking his eyes from what he was reading, he reached round, felt upon his plate for a scrap of kipper and fed it to the waiting cat.

Lady Agatha looked on approvingly and did not scold him for it. The cat licked its whiskers and sidled out.

"Ahem." Prudence looked hopefully at the thin leather binding of the treatise. The man behind it did not respond.

Perhaps he was not truly awake. Yes, he was in the room, he was sitting up, he was even respectably attired in a long dressing gown of black silk that went astonishingly well with his tousled black hair—but he was not really there.

"My dear, it is no use talking to Alwyn until he has had several cups of strong coffee," Lady Agatha said amiably. "Consider yourself lucky to see him at all. He is usually at the site of the library before daybreak and has his breakfast from the pieman. For some reason, he is favoring us with his company today."

"Is there coffee, Mama?"

"No."

Lord Alwyn harrumphed. "I should not drink it. I did not sleep well last night." In truth, he had tossed and turned until dawn, plagued by dreams of a certain young lady in lace-trimmed pantaloons and very little else.

"The Reverend Ponsonby considers it an unwholesome drink," Lady Agatha said.

Lord Alwyn looked around the architectural treatise to scowl at Prudence, who smiled at him anyway. "Did you invite him to breakfast, Mama? Must I keep hearing his name?"

"No, but I was thinking of inviting him to dinner. And the bishop as well. I thought I might serve beefsteak."

Her son yawned. "Serve him gruel. Ponsonby's ridiculous schemes have eaten up enough of your money."

"He is a great humanitarian, Alwyn," said Lady Agatha in a nettled way. "I am proud that his words are upon the cornerstone of my library."

"Do you mean that nonsense about oysters and pearls? There ought to be a law against such metaphors, in my opinion. Unless those who create them willy-nilly can be suitably trained—perhaps licensed."

Prudence stifled a giggle as Lady Agatha threw her son an exasperated look. "You are so critical, Alwyn! Do you think that your excellent education sets you above all other men?"

"In Ponsonby's case, certainly."

The old lady drew her robes around her and sulked until he spoke again.

"But I do think your library—and it is your library, not his—is a worthy cause." His tone was more than a little patronizing. Prudence could not blame Lady Agatha for being offended.

"Hm. Speaking of the library, you must get there before noon. The building cannot proceed without you, according to that man Herrick," Lady Agatha said. "He came to inquire as to your whereabouts a little while ago, just as we were coming down. He was wearing very dirty clothes. Broderick sent him away."

Alwyn glared at her. "You did not tell me that, Mama. I wonder what has happened."

"Pooh," said Lady Agatha. "Nothing of consequence. His accent is thick and his speech is quite common. He said something about bricks. Or mortar. Or stone. I cannot remember."

"Most buildings are constructed of these materials, my dear Mama," Alwyn said. "And the loftiest library requires the labor of common men."

Lady Agatha adjusted her turban and squinted at him over her spectacles. "But why must common men stand in my front hall in muddy boots?"

Alwyn rolled his eyes. "My dear Miss Reese, pray keep in mind that my mother is a believer in social equality and the rights of man. She just does not like mud in her hall."

"You left out the rights of women," his mother complained.

"Forgive me. But think a little harder. What did Herrick say?"

"To the best of my recollection, that there had been a 'hunfortunate hincident'—and that you should come sooner rather than later."

"Mama! You should certainly have told me that! Do you want the library to be completed on time?"

"Of course I do! The young women of London—"

"Must be served. I know." He threw an exasperated look at Prudence, who deemed it wise to stay out of this squabble, as she had stayed out of the one at the dinner table the night before.

"Well, if you wish to meet Herrick, you cannot

dawdle over breakfast, Alwyn. Go. Get dressed. Shall we see you at dinner?"

"No."

Ignoring the curtness of his reply, Lady Agatha turned up her cup until it nearly covered her nose, taking the last drop of tea with evident satisfaction.

The old dame's manners were a comical mixture of elegance and rudeness, Prudence thought. And her strong-willed son was more than a match for her.

Lady Agatha set her cup precisely in the middle of its saucer and rose from her chair, sweeping her silk robe about her considerable person with a flourish. "Prudence, we shall resume the cataloguing of the books within an hour. Beginning with A, of course."

Alwyn tossed the treatise down on the table with a resounding smack. "Why not start in the middle? Begin with M, then leap to X. And back to B." He regretted his sarcasm the second he spoke, but he could not take it back. Fatigue, irritation, and—he had to admit it—physical frustration were getting the better of him.

He cast his mind back to the moment he had first seen Miss Reese. Nothing in his otherwise well-ordered life had been the same since.

"Whatever is the matter with you?" Lady Agatha snapped. "We take our work seriously even if you do not."

He sighed with exaggerated patience. "My apologies to you, Mama. And to Miss Reese. But you do have the easiest part of this project, sitting about, dusting old books and taking naps. I am glad indeed that you have Prudence's help, however. Get through the remaining twenty-five letters in whatever order you wish."

"How very kind of you, Alwyn. We shall do just that."

Alwyn thought a moment. "Have you looked into adding the books I mentioned? The plays? The poetry? The fairy tales?"

His mother shook her head, which caused her grand turban to fall over one eye, giving her a disreputable air. But her voice was charged with her usual authority. "I have not changed my mind. Your suggestions were most unsuitable. And there is no more money until dividend day. We are relying on donations now."

And deadly dull they were, thought Prudence. "I might earn some," she said suddenly.

"What?" Lord Alwyn and Lady Agatha said in unison.

"There must be a way," Prudence replied.

"It is not done, my dear," the old lady said firmly. "You cannot sell ribbons behind a counter, you know. It simply is not done."

"But I must do something. You have been very kind, Lady Agatha, but I do not like to be dependent upon anyone for money. And my gowns and all that—"

"But we have not bought you any gowns," Lady Agatha pointed out. "And you have been a very great help to me. Surely you do not think, my dear, that you must contribute anything other than your charming company and invaluable assistance—" She wheezed and broke off, looking unhappily at Prudence.

"It is Ponsonby who is costing too much," said Lord Alwyn coldly. "He billed your solicitors over a thousand pounds for his expenses, you know."

Lady Agatha looked at him through narrowed eyes. "I am sure every penny will be accounted for."

"I am equally sure that it will not."

Prudence held up a hand. "Please listen. If I could earn my living in some way appropriate to my station—well, I think it would be a very good thing."

"But what could you possibly do?" Lord Alwyn inquired.

The scarlet-bound romance Prudence had hidden flashed into her mind. "I—I could write."

"Write?" Mother and son spoke in unison again.

"Yes, why not?"

Lord Alwyn could not help but smile. "I suppose you mean books, Miss Reese. Well, if you do not think there are enough of those in this house, then feel free to add another one or two to the mountain."

"Alwyn!" the old lady scolded him again. "Do not speak so rudely! I applaud Miss Reese's desire for financial independence. My father and yours made sure that I was provided for in my old age, but that is not true in every case. If Prudence wishes to write, she shall begin today."

"Thank you, Lady Agatha," Prudence murmured. The Purcells sometimes seemed willing to quarrel about anything at all. She would not give them any encouragement. "I was thinking of writing a novel."

"Aha!" Lord Alwyn grinned in that wolfish way of his. "A romance? You must put in swoons, sweet talk, and enough heartfelt sighs to blow a full-rigged ship across the Atlantic."

Prudence tried to maintain an unruffled air. How on earth did he know she was thinking of writing a romance? Had he found the scarlet-bound tale of Pamela Jones hidden in the rooms above and assumed as much?

She had not been able to explain the drawings he had taken away inside his shirt. He must think that she had similar pictures and scandalous novels squirreled away in other hidey-holes.

"You are insufferable," Lady Agatha said. "Prudence would never write such trash."

Lord Alwyn raised his thick black brows in an expression of mock astonishment. "You never know. I find that Miss Reese is full of surprises."

"My dear Prudence, forgive him. My son is entirely too full of himself. I cannot imagine why. He matriculated at the finest university in Edinburgh, has taken the Grand Tour twice, has perfect taste, and knows everything."

"Thank you, Mama. Since I am such a paragon, Miss Reese can model the hero of her story on me." He turned to show his profile and struck a suitably noble pose in his armchair. "How do I look?"

"Hmph. Like a villain," Lady Agatha retorted. "Especially in that black robe."

"Excellent," he said. "The villain usually gets to do what he wants for pages and pages. Heroes have to wave swords and rescue silly maidens and be drearily splendid at all times."

"There is rather more to a hero than that," Lady Agatha said crisply.

"Of course, Mama. I was only joking. I did not mean to upset you or your turban. I do apologize."

The old lady straightened it. "Well, then. I forgive you."

Lord Alwyn smiled and it occurred to Prudence that his bickering with his mother had an affectionate undertone that had escaped her at first.

She was less sure of how he felt about her. He did not seem overly impressed by her idea for employment.

Even she had to admit that it was half-baked, impulsively voiced, and might never come to pass. But he could have been a trifle more gallant and a trifle less toplofty, certainly.

Would Lord Alwyn only admire her if she stood like a statue in an empty niche and looked pretty enough to catch his eye for a fleeting moment? That would never satisfy her. She could not tell him that, of course. Perhaps it would have been best if they had never met.

Life in the Purcell household had been safe enough—and altogether predictable—until that moment. Everything seemed to have changed when he kissed her upon the stairs.

Her mother's plans to marry her off, Lady Agatha's do-gooding, her own vague notions of what the future might bring—all had seemed to vanish at the touch of his lips.

She had hoped it would happen again. Her wish had almost come true, thanks to Marmalady. Chasing the cat had brought them together again in an almost indecent way. And when Alwyn found the hidden pictures—oh, dear. It was clear that their encounters were going from bad to worse, and that the worst was yet to come.

The object of her reverie snapped his fingers and brought her back to the present moment. "Miss Reese! Are you already plotting this immortal work of literature?"

"N-no," she stammered.

"Then what are you plotting? You seem to be a million miles away."

"Your immediate demise, perhaps," Lady Agatha said crossly.

He waved away this jibe. "Let us consider the other aspects of Miss Reese's startling announcement," he said. "Will pretty pictures be required for this story? I know just the artist."

Prudence ignored this pointed remark and the wink that accompanied it. "I have not given that much thought to it. In truth, I have no idea what I will write about—but I shall start today. All I need is paper, pen, and ink."

Lady Agatha clapped her hands. "And a dear little desk! We shall browse to our heart's content upon Tottenham Court Road and buy secondhand to save on expense." She thought for another moment and cast a sly glance at her son. "It must have locks, to keep your magnum opus safe from prying eyes."

"Humph. I suppose you mean me, Mama. Rest assured that I will always respect Miss Reese's privacy." This was true, but he would perish of curiosity nonetheless. He returned to his architectural treatise just in time to escape his mother's dismissive look.

"Come, Prudence. We have a reason to escape and a fine day on which to do so." She attached herself to her young relation's arm. "Tra-la! We are going shopping!"

Alwyn simply shrugged. "Enjoy yourselves. Miss Reese, perhaps you are a literary genius—or might become one. But writing is tedious work. Have you sufficient patience? A good imagination? You lack experience of the world, you know."

His superior tone piqued her. "I will find out what I need to know somehow," she replied, a tinge of tartness in her voice.

He raised an eyebrow. "Then I look forward to seeing the finished book upon a shelf of *my* magnum opus—the Purcell Library. And I offer you a challenge. If I finish building before you finish the book, you must dedicate it to our dissolute Prince Regent."

"Alwyn, you don't mean that—do you?" his mother asked. She looked at him, then at Prudence.

He shook his head. "Of course not, Mama. I am merely trying to annoy you."

Prudence rose from her chair and cast a proud look at him. "A race to the finish might be amusing. But your challenge is hardly fair. You have many men to help you, whereas I must work alone."

"Scribbling a book should be easy enough," Alwyn said indifferently.

"Have you ever done it?" she asked.

"No, of course not."

"I shall write a good one, sir," she said boldly. "But your library will be only as good as the books it holds. Without them it will be no more than a mere box of bricks."

He considered her words for a moment. "Well said, Miss Reese."

The defiant tilt of her chin and the fire in her gorgeous blue eyes at that moment made taking his next breath difficult. He did like a woman with spirit, and, as he had learned at their first meeting, Miss Reese did not like to be cornered.

What was it Charles had said so offhandedly? That Alwyn would meet his match someday?

He realized suddenly that he had. But he could not quite think of the proper word for the intense emotion that seemed to have stopped his heart for a fraction of a second.

Love? Pshaw.

She glared at him fiercely. Those eyes were incomparable.

Admiration. Perhaps that was what he was feeling. Unbelievably intense admiration. He was willing to believe that at least. After all, he hardly knew her and he was a stranger to true love, in any case—

Do shut up, he told himself, looking away first. Such things took time, and no genuine feeling happened of an instant. His attraction to her was a passing fancy, that was all.

Alwyn was silently grateful for the presence of his mother. Otherwise he might do something rash, like declare himself. Carry her off to the nearest overstuffed article of furniture and teach her those things she did not know. Marry her the very next day and be happy for the rest of his life.

"Alwyn!" his mother barked. "You are staring at Miss Reese in the oddest way. Come to your senses!"

He gathered his wits. "Yes, Mama."

"Well?" Prudence said rather rudely. "Do you wish to say more?"

Damnation. Had Cupid struck him with a poisoned arrow? Her impertinence alone ought to be enough to bring him to his senses.

He was a thoughtful man—a man of reason, as he often said—with none of his mother's unfortunate impulsiveness. He would think it over, perhaps ask Charles for advice—no, Charles would gossip. Alwyn tapped his fingers upon the breakfast table and spoke in measured tones.

"Miss Reese, building a library is a much more complex task than merely writing a book—and it is not as if I could do it myself. But will the book you plan to write endure? My library will stand for a century or more."

His mother let out a little shriek. "That was what Herrick said! I remember now! It has tumbled down!"

Chapter Eight

To be precise, one wall of it had fallen down. Alwyn heaved a sigh of relief as he approached the construction site, kicking up dust as he ran. A knot of workmen stood near a heap of broken bricks and lumber, looking closely at the jagged edges that remained.

He went to them. "Good God! I should have done the calculations immediately! Was anyone hurt?"

Herrick tipped his cap. "No, sir. It came down 'afore the men were up on the scaffold. Look 'ere." He pointed and Alwyn saw a trickle of water bubbling through the mud near their feet. "There were a buried spring, and water will find its way. The foundation settled and cracked, and that 'as brought the wall down."

"Damnation! This will set us back several weeks. The source of the spring must be discovered and its flow diverted before we can rebuild."

Herrick nodded. "Me brother builds dams and such in Henley-on-Thames. I sent a lad there on the one o'clock coach to fetch 'im."

"There is nothing more we can do. We must call a halt to construction until he arrives."

"Yes, sir. The men could work at yer mother's 'ouse in the meantime," Herrick pointed out.

Lord Alwyn frowned—and then he smiled slowly. "A capital idea, come to think of it. Mama will be distracted by the incessant hammering and muddy footprints everywhere, and less inclined to argue with me." He supposed he ought to feel as destroyed as the wall that lay in rubble at his feet, but oddly enough, he did not.

"Beggin' yer pardon, sir?"

"Give me a moment to think, Herrick." He clasped his hands behind his back and walked around the perimeter of the site, thinking not about the building at all, but about Miss Reese.

Supervising the remaining construction at his mama's house, if only for a day or two, would give him many opportunities to talk to Prudence. If his mama retired to her room with a headache from the noise, so much the better.

Of course, should the entire library fall down no matter what they did, he could spend an entire year at Purcell House redesigning his magnum opus in Prudence's pleasant company. He would need at least that long to think about the brief moment that had shaken him so.

Naturally, he would not share these irrational thoughts with Herrick. They were only thoughts.

He came full circle to where the master builder was standing.

Herrick gave him a puzzled look. "Sir, what were you saying about Lady Agatha?"

"Never mind. My dear mama likes to have things her way, that is all."

"Nothing wrong wif t'at, sir." Herrick stood by patiently as Alwyn jotted down a list.

"Assign the carpenters and bricklayers to the areas of her town house that remain unfinished—the dormer rooms for the servants and the back garden wall, to start. Then rope off this site and set two men on watch to keep the street urchins out of it."

Herrick tipped his cap again. "Very good, sir."

A hearty slap on the back from an unseen person caused Alwyn to drop his pencil and paper. "Told you so," Charles Sudbury said affably, stepping forth and surveying the wreckage. "Why didn't you listen?"

"Because you were drunk, my dear friend."

"But I was right."

Alwyn gritted his teeth. "Yes. You were. Had I used my head and done the calculations, I would have been able to confirm your suspicions."

"The problem could be seen with the naked eye. My naked eye, anyway."

"I prefer to measure."

Charles guffawed. "Then do it. Or we'll end up with a leaning tower like that Italian one. Or a twisty-turny ziggurat. Interestin' structures, ziggurats. The ancient Babylonians were quite fond of 'em. So why didn't you measure yesterday?"

Alwyn felt his face flush. "Blast the Babylonians! I could not because . . . because I fell ill after I sent you home."

Another slap on the back made him stagger. "Heard about the Billingsgate basket," Charles laughed. "Wouldn't mind riding in the contraption myself. Never know what you might see in a boudoir window, eh?"

Alwyn scowled. "The basket has been returned."

"A pity." Hands clasped behind his back, Charles walked away to inspect the fallen wall and talk to the workmen.

"Will there be anything else, sir?" Herrick asked.

"See that Charles doesn't fall down a hidden well.

Though sometimes I wish he would, no matter that he is my dearest friend, and a brilliant architect."

It was Herrick's turn to grin. "I will look after 'im, sir. Will there be anything else?"

"Yes. Dispatch a messenger to my house so that my mother knows things are not as bad as I thought. I will explain the details to Miss Reese myself—Mama is not interested in such things."

A few hours later . . .

Wandering through jumbled stacks of furniture was a pleasant diversion, as the secondhand store was blissfully quiet. Lord Alwyn—who seemed to want to talk to her, though Prudence did not want to talk to him—had informed them personally of the extent of the damage at the library and sent his workmen to Lady Agatha's house, where they were now making an unbearable racket.

Trailed by a footman, who twirled his hat in his hand with a bored air, Lady Agatha and Prudence dawdled and deliberated over one desk after another.

The old lady rejected several sturdy walnut desks as too ugly and therefore likely to inhibit creativity, and a whimsical one of faux bamboo as too rickety.

Prudence spotted the perfect desk at last. Painted robin's-egg blue, it had ingeniously wrought cubbyholes, a wide, smooth writing surface, and numerous drawers that locked.

The matching chair was in need of a leg, but the elderly shopkeeper promised to add this and reduced the price at Lady Agatha's insistence. She then arranged for the footmen to supervise its delivery.

"You shall pen a masterpiece at this, my dear," said

Lady Agatha feelingly. "The color blue is stimulating to the intellect."

"I did not know that," Prudence said. "But it is very pretty and will certainly do." She looked it over one last time, opening and closing the drawers to make sure they worked smoothly, finding an elegant pen in one and a carved mother-of-pearl button in another.

"There! It once belonged to a lady. Perhaps she wrote at it as well," Lady Agatha smiled.

"I shall use her pen—and keep the button for luck," Prudence declared.

The desk arrived in the early evening. Lady Agatha and Prudence were ready for it, having spent the intervening time making room in Prudence's bedroom. Cathy, who had been posted at the stairs, heard the footmen arrive downstairs.

Marmalady could also be heard. She expressed her indignation over this new disturbance with plaintive meows and refused to budge. With her and her kittens inside, the wardrobe was to be moved, per Lady Agatha's instructions, six inches to the left.

Cathy watched as Broderick put a muscular shoulder to its side and gave a powerful shove into place. The butler straightened and clapped imaginary dust off his hands as if his effort had been nothing at all. He frowned when he saw that the red-haired maid was no longer looking at him.

Step by step, the footmen hauled the blue desk up the stairs between them. They negotiated the turns with anxious instructions from Lady Agatha, a few steps behind them, who waved a handkerchief and generally made a nuisance of herself.

"It is of utmost importance that it not be scratched! Turn left! Go right! Hold it higher!"

Prudence sighed. Despite their grunts, the footmen were managing well enough. As always, Lady Agatha could scarcely contain her excitement over a new passion. It seemed that the notion of Prudence becoming an author truly tickled her.

The dear old lady meant well, but the thought of her hovering over the desk as Prudence wrote was disconcerting. Add to that the challenge that Lord Alwyn had offered—she would *not* dedicate her first book to the Prince Regent, and that was that—and Prudence was nervous indeed.

She was sure that she could write a better book than *The Persuasion of Pamela Jones*—or could she? Her unworldliness might well prove a stumbling block, as Lord Alwyn had pointed out.

Obviously, her novel would need to be rich in wisdom and erudition, with finely drawn characters and a masterful plot, if she was to impress a man educated at the finest university in Edinburgh.

She would need to read other novels. And philosophy. And poetry. And satire. And perhaps a romance or two. There must be a reason those were so wildly popular, no matter what the learned Lord Alwyn thought of them.

Fortunately, they had passed Mr. Furnivall's shop in Chiswell Street on the way home. The bookseller, Lady Agatha's dear friend, had the largest selection in London, according to her. They had not gone in, but Prudence was given to understand that Mr. Furnivall was a friendly old fellow and she might do so at any time.

Prudence returned her attention to the matter at hand. Once the footmen and the desk and last of all, Lady Agatha, had passed the second landing, she took her skirts in hand to follow them.

She did not see Lord Alwyn enter through the door that had been left open, nor did she see his approving look at her ankles. She scampered up the stairs and out of sight.

Alwyn sighed as he watched her go. She had not been as interested in the repair and rebuilding plans as he had hoped—but that was to be expected, as her talents were of another sort. A writer, as she hoped to be, built pretty castles in the air with but a flick of a pen, not immense boxes of brick requiring the arduous labor of a hundred men.

She did have a way with words. He would have to be on guard against that. Intelligence plus beauty plus feminine charm plus—oh, everything else, she had it all—might prove to be irresistible. But a battle of wits with dear Miss Reese ought to be an even match, should it come to pass. He would have to brush up his *bon mots* and ripostes, just in case.

He had not been in best form this morning. He hoped she had not been offended by his rather rude suggestion for a race to the finish: Library vs. Book. He had retracted the challenge immediately when pressed by his mama.

Lord Alwyn peered up the stairs, hoping Prudence would return. There was no sound of her or anyone else. He would be climbing the stairs soon enough and falling into bed. His lack of sleep and the difficulties at the building site had tired him more than he wanted to admit.

As the day wore on, it had become clear that correcting the cause of the wall's collapse would call for both great ingenuity and additional expense they could ill afford at this stage.

The workmen at his mother's house would have to finish quickly and return to the site, where they were needed immediately. Just digging to the source of the spring would take at least a week. Such hidden water was a common enough occurrence, according to Herrick's brother. This part of London, built upon land partly reclaimed from the Thames, had many underground streams.

Lord Alwyn was more than tired; he was exhausted. But that flash of white stockings had cheered him up nonetheless. Miss Reese had very nice ankles indeed.

He set his hat upon the chiffomonster in the hall and picked up the bill of sale left upon its marble top. *One desk, painted blue,* it read. *Chair to be mended and delivered tomorrow.*

So Miss Reese was determined to become an author. Why not? He realized that he had been somewhat condescending on the subject and regretted that he had upset her. He cared not a whit whether she finished her book, and she could dedicate to the devil for all he cared. She might do as she pleased; he would be happy simply to be near her.

Prudence had signed the bill of sale, not Lady Agatha. He traced a finger over the feminine curves of her fine script and sighed, feeling deliciously silly.

No woman had ever affected him in quite this way. Every little thing about her was damnably attractive, from her pretty white stockings to her handwriting.

As far he knew, such stupidity over trifles, such joy at the sight of mere ankles, was known as . . . love.

He reminded himself that what he was experiencing was no more than unbelievably intense admiration.

He wondered whether she had any feelings for him. Would Miss Reese even consider a younger son, penniless as she was? This was an extremely prickly question.

Prudence chose that moment to return for the bill and saw him standing there when she was halfway down the stairs.

Oho. Judging by the expression on his face, he thought they had paid too much. He seemed determined to disapprove of this project but that would not stop her. Head held high, she skipped down the last three stairs and took the bill from his hand.

"Miss Reese!"

"We paid less than half a crown. It was a bargain. The desk is most ingeniously made."

Alwyn nodded graciously. "I do hope it is not as ornate as the chiffomonster." He tapped a finger upon the marble slab where his hat rested. "One such piece is enough for me. I have often explained the principles of good taste to mama, but she seems not to listen and simply buys what she likes."

"Have you forgotten that this is her house?" Prudence said.

"No—of course not. You are quite right, Miss Reese."

Her belligerent expression was rather comical. Still, it would not do to mock whatever item of furniture she had bought. He had not seen it yet . . . and she might think again that he did not take her literary aspirations seriously.

Alwyn took a few seconds to admire the brightness of her eyes before he spoke again. "I see that the desk is blue." That was a safe enough thing to say, surely.

She glared at him. "What of it?"

"Miss Reese, I only meant to say—" He broke off. What *had* he meant to say?

Your eyes are a blue far more beautiful than the damned desk, Miss Reese. Your cheeks are pink and your stockings are white and I can see more of your bosom than is good for me, Miss Reese. My lonely heart is on fire for you. Worst of all, you make me run out of adjectives—and I feel like a fool.

He took a deep breath. "I meant to say that I approve of your choice."

"I did not ask for your approval."

He looked directly at her, making no secret of his annoyance. "Forgive me. I was only trying to be pleasant."

She seemed somewhat mollified. "Well, then. Would you like to come see it? Your mama is supervising its installation in my bedroom."

"Certainly." His annoyance vanished. "Are we friends again?"

She smiled in reply and her pretty chin tilted up. "Yes."

Damn the girl. Her smile was positively irresistible. But he would *not* tell her the truth, not yet. Which was that he had no desire whatsoever to be her friend. He had wanted to kiss her within a minute of their first meeting . . . he had wanted to kiss her upon the roof . . . and when they were briefly alone in her bedroom . . . and he wanted to kiss her now.

He ought to be capable of self-restraint, he thought, amazed at the strength of his desire for her. He was older, more patient, knew that he should be quite sure of his feelings for dearest Pru—*dearest Miss Reese*, he corrected himself silently—before he did something they both might regret.

On second thought, he had done himself out of two wonderful kisses in less than two days. This could not go on. There was no reason to be too reasonable.

"Prudence," he said slowly. "That does not seem like the right name for you. You are impetuous. And—passionate."

Her lips parted with surprise. If that was not an invitation to a kiss, his name was not—

"Alwyn!"

Blast! His dear mama was waddling down the stairs. She was looking back at the footmen following her and had not seen the almost-kiss. He hoped.

Prudence went to Lady Agatha when she reached the first floor to give her the bill of sale.

"What is this? Oh, never mind." The old lady gave it a glance and put it into Alwyn's hat, then thought better of it and tucked the bill into a nook in the chiffomonster instead.

"I promise to repay you as soon as possible, Lady Agatha," Prudence said.

"Tut-tut. Certainly not, my dear. You need other things. We must go to the stationer tomorrow and procure a ream of paper. And a blotter." She put her finger to her chin. "Scissors. Ink. Nibs. Sealing wax. And wrapping paper and twine so we may send your magnum opus promptly to a publisher."

Prudence laughed merrily. "I have not written a word!"

"But you will, Miss Reese," Lord Alwyn said. "I wish you success. I know you will achieve it." He picked up his hat, and made an elegant bow.

Lady Agatha watched him go upstairs, and then

turned to Prudence. "Well! He *has* changed his tune. How did you do it, my girl?"

Wide-eyed, Prudence looked at her. She had not the slightest idea.

Two mornings later, Lady Agatha was working in her study, sitting at a desk that was a relic of a more fanciful era in design. Alwyn called it rococo—it was decorated with dizzying spirals and cockleshells in gilt on white.

He hated it. She loved it. And that was what counted.

Dear boy, she thought indulgently. He wanted everything to be elegant, serene, and uncluttered. That was certainly not how she liked her rooms decorated.

In this room, her fanciful taste was freely expressed. Porcelain shepherdesses fought for space upon the crowded shelves with Staffordshire dogs. The dogs seemed to be winning—they outnumbered the delicate shepherdesses two to one.

A japanned screen inlaid with mother-of-pearl leaned somewhat crookedly against the wallpaper, upon which were pasted exotic birds cut from an old book. Her handiwork, of course—and she had not been careful with the paste, which could be seen in places. But the effect was amusing, Lady Agatha thought.

The *pièce de résistance* was a statue of Bacchus—a Greek original, according to Alwyn, who said it was antique and quite valuable. The marble god of good times lolled about in an arbor of marble grapes, looking dissolute and cheerful. Lady Agatha had tied a flowered scarf about his middle to cover up his naughty bits should clergymen come to call.

She had thousands of things and she loved them all. Alwyn often poked fun at the accumulation of strange objects but she rarely listened to his lectures on good taste.

Perhaps Prudence's presence would mellow him. She sensed a strong attraction between them, and Alwyn was at the age where a man ought to marry. She supposed he had grown up as much as he was going to.

In her opinion, Prudence was perfect. Surely her son was bright enough to seize the day, not to mention the lady, and not wait forever. Of course, Lady Agatha would need to delay her young relation's debut. She would simply not mention it for the time being—that would be easy enough.

If Prudence were to be swept up into the social whirl, she would undoubtedly have any number of admirers. If she were to stay close to home, that would better Alwyn's chances of winning her hand.

She looked out the window and thought it over once more. Her son and Prudence would need time alone now and then. As his mama, her nearly constant presence in the house would provide the necessary appearance of decorum. But Lady Agatha was good at disappearing when the moment seemed right—and reappearing when propriety demanded it.

Did they think she had not noticed when they went upon the roof to rescue Marmalady's kitten? Did they not know that it was a mother's gift to observe without seeming to do so at all?

She smiled and put down her pen to look at the birds. Scared away by Herrick's men, they had returned in force today—a parliament of sparrows and starlings twittered outside her study window.

She was glad that the work at her house had been completed so quickly. Lady Agatha did not miss the mud the men tracked in during their brief sojourn at Purcell House, nor their rough shouts and annoying racket. But they had provided entertainment in their own way, hanging upside down in windows and begging her pardon very politely when they gave her a start.

She enjoyed their mischief—a thought that put her in mind of grandchildren. It was time for Alwyn to think along similar lines. Her first son never would.

Chapter Nine

Two months later . . .

"Prooo-dence!"

"Yes, Lady Agatha?"

Sitting at her blue desk, her back very straight, Prudence looked at her bedroom door, which was locked.

"How goes your magnum opus, my dear?"

"Oh—very well."

"Then carry on." Lady Agatha's footsteps receded down the hall.

Prudence stared hopelessly at the piece of paper before her. It was smooth. It was white. It was blank. She still had not written a word.

How fortunate it was that Lady Agatha thought it best to leave her alone. The old dear had no way of knowing that Prudence had done nothing at all in the weeks since the desk's arrival, though she had tried. Oh, how she had tried!

Whenever she heard Lady Agatha's halloos and cheery inquiries as to her progress, Prudence would make the old chair creak and scratch her dry quill against the blotter before hallooing back. She could not imagine what other noise a writer might make.

Frustrated groans, perhaps.

Though she sat faithfully at the desk for two hours every morning, the Muse did not visit her and creative lightning did not strike.

Her lack of progress was entirely her own fault **and she** could not say that she was distracted. As **her bedroom** was situated on the opposite side of the house, which faced away from the library site, the sounds of construction and the shouts of the workmen were muffled. Still, she knew perfectly well that Lord Alwyn's magnum opus was coming along splendidly, thanks to Lady Agatha.

She was proud of her second son, even if she had said that his chosen profession was not quite gentlemanly, and she bragged often of the library to anyone who would listen. Yet the old lady was also proud of Prudence. A regular visitor to the stationer's shop, she continued to procure every small thing that her young relation might need: quills by the score, bottles of ink, and even a brass paperweight in the shape of a hedgehog.

Prudence spent much time fiddling with these but not writing. She picked up the carved mother-of-pearl button that had belonged to the desk's previous owner and rubbed it for luck.

Not that luck had anything to do with producing an actual book, of course. It had been the height of foolishness on her part to suppose that it was easy, just because she had read so many boring, badly written ones while assisting Lady Agatha.

With a wry smile, Prudence recalled her dream last night: the paper, pens, and ink had magically produced sentences, paragraphs, and chapters all on their own, with no human hand to guide them. Blast! She hated to admit it but Lord Alwyn had been right. She lacked patience and she lacked inspiration.

Worst of all, she still lacked money of her own. Her dependence upon the kindness of Lady Agatha troubled her more and more, even if that dear lady offered every assurance that Prudence might stay at Purcell House indefinitely.

At least Lady Agatha had not mentioned her debut for weeks, much to Prudence's relief. It was a costly and unnecessary introduction to a society that would think little of a penniless young woman anyway.

She wondered just how much the author of a successful novel earned, then wondered if it was crass of her to think of money.

A deep sigh escaped her. Was not writing an art? The highest expression of the human soul? But she knew she was unlikely to pen deathless prose. Would it be all right if readers simply found her story entertaining and nothing more?

Prudence reminded herself that she had *no* story of any kind and chewed fretfully on the end of her pen.

When asked for his opinion on the matter, Lord Alwyn had simply shrugged his shoulders and said he had not the slightest idea. He had been somewhat distant in the last weeks.

Perhaps it was because of the library. He seemed to think of little else and was seldom at Purcell House during the days.

Accordingly, she had too much time to sit alone and no one to flirt with. Perhaps his suggestion to model the hero on him was hindering her. No doubt he had forgotten his flippant remark, but she had not.

It was far too easy to imagine him in a romantic novel with his dark hair and good looks and his penchant for stealing kisses, but she could not put any of that on paper for his mama to read.

Unfortunately, she knew of no other man who might do in his place. She picked up a new quill, ran its feathery edge through her fingers, and moved the brass hedgehog to this place and that.

She wondered what he had done with the drawings of the amorous couple. He had not said one word about them. Mayhap he had taken them back to his other apartments, though he always slept at Purcell House now.

With nothing left to wonder about, she reached into a cubbyhole and pulled out the most recent letter from her own dear mama. Lady Felicia had inquired rather rudely as to her debut; she had heard nothing of it for weeks, and threatened a prolonged visit.

She had been effectively stalled by a return post from Lady Agatha, who explained that the household was overrun by rapidly growing kittens that no one could bear to part with. This was not a lie. Thanks to Prudence, Lady Agatha knew that cats made Lady Felicia sneeze until her face turned red. Prudence's mama was justly proud of her milk-white complexion and would surely stay away.

Prudence let out a prodigious sigh, bored beyond belief. Whatever had made her think that she could write a novel? She was shut up in this house for hours each day, saw no one, did not go out in society and knew nothing of love. She knew a little about her own sex, but men were a mystery and Lord Alwyn was no exception.

She had few diversions, except a trip now and

then to the top floor, which offered a partial view of the library. As the site itself was a sea of mud, according to Lady Agatha, Prudence avoided it when she walked out, not wishing to bedraggle her skirts—or to seem overly interested.

Most of the books destined for the library had been put into one category or another, though Prudence still thought it would be simplest to divide them into Dull and Duller. Fortunately, Lady Agatha had enlisted Cathy as her assistant for the nonce. She found the girl bright and trustworthy, and Prudence was glad to be relieved of this irksome chore.

She had not looked at the library for several days—perhaps she would climb out upon the roof to get a better view, though she would have to be careful not to tear or dirty her dress. Then she would have something to say about it should Lord Alwyn appear at dinner tonight.

The walls and the roof were nearly complete, she knew that much. Mr. Herrick's brother had seen to the temporary diversion of the spring and laid pipe to direct some of it to a fountain that would be installed in the center of the library courtyard.

The rest of the water would be directed along the sides of the building for a garden. Alwyn had regaled them not long ago with details of its irrigation, the placement of rain gutters and so forth. Prudence had tried not to be envious of his progress.

His magnum opus was coming along swimmingly, while hers was not. She could not even come up with so much as an opening line for her non-existent book, because she knew nothing.

No, that was not quite true. Her recent evening in Alwyn's company had taught her much about drains, but that information could not be easily worked into a novel, and it lacked drama.

Botheration. What did other authoresses write about? Love? War? Pudding recipes?

She would have to visit the Chiswell Street shop and buy every single one of her female competitors' books. Mr. Furnivall would certainly approve.

"Romances? Which ones?" the bookseller asked patiently. He tucked a large repeating watch in the pocket of his yellow brocade waistcoat and tried not to look like the busy man he was.

"All of them. I must begin somewhere and love is an interesting subject. At least I find it interesting."

"Most ladies do," Mr. Furnivall sighed. "But we have two thousand, six hundred and forty-seven romances upon these shelves, according to—"

He was interrupted by a gray little woman of indeterminate age whom Prudence had not seen until that moment. "That number is not correct. We sold seven romances yesterday, but the customer returned two. There are two thousand, six hundred and forty-two romances upon the shelves."

"Miss Reese, allow me to introduce Miss Sparks, my assistant."

Prudence smiled eagerly. "I do hope you will be able to help me, Miss Sparks. I want to write a book but I don't know where to begin."

The assistant simply stared like an owl as her employer spoke for her.

"As well as keeping a precise count of all our titles, Miss Sparks is a grammarian of genius. Should you have any questions regarding definitions, syntax, typographical composition or punctuation, ask her. A well-placed comma is her greatest joy. But you must excuse me—a customer approaches!"

The bookseller moved behind the counter as a well-dressed man came up to it, his arms laden with expensive new books.

Miss Sparks beckoned and Prudence followed her to another part of the store.

The gray woman stopped suddenly in the middle of an aisle and pointed left and right. "Look anywhere in this section if it is romance you want. I have arranged them in alphabetical order but the customers *will* put them back wrong—it is extremely irritating."

"I understand," murmured Prudence sympathetically.

"And sometimes the authors come in and turn their books face out, high up, where they can be seen. As if I don't notice! I have seen a certain bishop—a very great man, dressed all in black—put copies of his book on particular display in the theology section. Over there." She pointed to a far shelf. "Eggy had to put them back properly, spines out."

Prudence raised her eyebrows and tried to look shocked.

"The bishop buys copies of his own work, so it will seem that it sells well. If *he* can be so wicked—well, there is nothing more to say."

Prudence nodded. "Oh, quite."

"As I was saying, I like to keep everything in its proper place and I like to know exactly where things are at all times." She waved at the nearest shelf. "These are new."

There were hundreds, Prudence thought with

dismay. She would have to write a very exciting book indeed to compete with so many.

Miss Sparks pulled a book from the capacious pocket of her baggy gray dress and tucked it between others on a different shelf. "These are older titles, in their second and third printings."

"Which are the most popular?"

Miss Sparks stared at her again. "The most popular ones are not in the store. They have been sold, of course. That is how one knows they are popular." She repeated the word softly to herself, as if she liked the sound of it. "Popular."

The little assistant was really very odd, Prudence thought, but of course it took all sorts of people to make the world go 'round. She smiled at her courteously. "I see, Miss Sparks. Thank you for your help. I do appreciate it."

She ran a finger idly over the rows of books as the gray woman moved away, her down-at-heel shoes making a *shush-shush* noise. Where to begin?

Without looking at titles, Prudence plucked two books from the shelves, simply because they were next to each other. She looked at the buckram cover of the first. *The Loves of Lady Lascivia*. That sounded fascinating.

She looked at the second—oh, no. *Moral Discourses* again? What was that doing here? Miss Sparks would not make the mistake of putting such a book upon the romance shelf.

And Bishop Applegate would expire of apoplexy if he knew he was cheek-to-cheek, so to speak, with *Lady Lascivia*.

The thing to do was put *Moral Discourses* back upon the shelf. In her haste, she dropped it—and

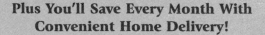

We'd Like to Invite You to Subscribe to Zebra's Regency Romance Book Club and Send You 4 Free Books as Your Introduction! (Worth $19.96!)

If you're a Regency lover, imagine the joy of getting **4 FREE Zebra Regency Romances** and then the chance to have these lovely stories delivered to your home each month at the lowest price available! Well, that's our offer to you and here's how you benefit by becoming a Regency Romance subscriber:

- *4 FREE Introductory Regency Romances are delivered to your doorstep (you only pay for shipping & handling)*

- *4 BRAND NEW Regencies are then delivered each month (usually before they're available in bookstores)*

- *Subscribers save almost $4.00 off the cover price every month*

- *You also receive a FREE monthly newsletter, which features author profiles, discounts, subscriber benefits, book previews and more*

- *There's no risks or obligations...in other words, you can cancel whenever you wish with no questions asked*

Join the thousands of readers who enjoy the savings and convenience offered to Regency Romance subscribers. After your initial introductory shipment, you'll receive 4 brand-new Zebra Regency Romances each month to examine for 10 days. Then, if you decide to keep the books, you pay the preferred subscriber's price, plus shipping and handling.

It's a no-lose proposition, so return the FREE BOOK CERTIFICATE today!

4 FREE BOOKS are waiting for you! Just mail in the certificate below!

to 4 Free Books!

Complete and return the order card to receive your FREE books, a $19.96 value!

FREE BOOK CERTIFICATE

YES! Please rush me 4 FREE Zebra Regency Romances (I only pay $1.99 for shipping and handling).I understand that each month thereafter I will be able to preview 4 brand-new Regency Romances FREE for 10 days. Then, if I should decide to keep them, I will pay the money-saving preferred subscriber's price for all 4... (that's a savings of 20% off the retail price), plus shipping and handling. I may return any shipment within 10 days and owe nothing, and I may cancel this subscription at any time.

Name _____

Address_____ Apt._____

City_____ State_____ Zip_____

Telephone (___)_____

Signature_____

(If under 18, parent or guardian must sign)

Offer limited to one per household and not to current subscribers. Terms, offer and prices subject to change. Orders subject to acceptance by Regency Romance Book Club. Offer Valid in the U.S. only.   RN053A

If the certificate is missing below, write to:

Regency Romance Book Club,
P.O. Box 5214,
Clifton, NJ 07015-5214

or call TOLL-FREE
1-800-770-1963

Visit our websitte at
www.kensingtonbooks.com

Treat yourself to 4 FREE Regency Romances!
A $19.96 VALUE… FREE!
No obligation to buy anything ever!

ll..l..lll...ll.l.l.l...l.l.l..ll.l.l..l.l.ll...l

REGENCY ROMANCE BOOK CLUB
Zebra Home Subscription Service, Inc.
P.O. Box 5214
Clifton NJ 07015-5214

out fell drawings very like the ones in Lady Agatha's copy.

But how had they come to be in this book? Were they the same? She looked for the mark that Lord Alwyn had showed her, indicating the number in the series, and found it.

These were the next five out of the fifteen! The couple in the garden were the same, but their positions were more frankly amorous in nature—yet not the least bit lewd. These drawings were even lovelier than the first she had found and she decided quickly to keep them.

She blushed scarlet and slid them back inside the book. Quite at random, wandering about the aisles, she chose an armful of other books and placed *Moral Discourses* on top and *Lady Lascivia* on the bottom, holding the stack in place with her chin as she walked to the counter.

"Are you ready, my dear?" Mr. Furnivall asked. "Did you find what you were looking for?"

She nodded as best she could, considering that she was using her chin to hold the bishop's book closed. "Yes, Miss Sparks was most helpful."

"Very good."

The old man took the stack from her and set it upon the counter, straightening the corners so that it would not topple. He made no comment, discreet or otherwise, on her choices. As he divided the stack in two, he gave her a benign smile that made her feel very guilty indeed.

"Thank you, Mr. Furnivall."

"So many! You have hours of pleasurable reading to look forward to, Miss Reese."

She gulped. "Y-yes. I suppose I do. Your selection is quite, um, select."

The bookseller nodded. "We pride ourselves upon that. And the shop lad will deliver them promptly."

He jotted down the prices and placed the books upon two sheets of paper, wrapping them carefully into parcels and tying them up with string.

"Egbert!" he called. "Egbert! That boy is never where he should be and he is always doing something he shouldn't. Eggy, where are you?"

The shop lad, a tall boy of seventeen or so, appeared and slouched against the counter. "I was unpacking them boxes of dictionaries, guv'nor. Wot next?" He favored Prudence with a cheeky grin and scratched his ear.

"Do not scratch in the presence of a lady. You are to deliver these to Lady Agatha's house. Do not dawdle in the streets and do not whistle at women."

The boy stood up straight. "I don't never do, sir."

"I have heard otherwise, Eggy. And that was a double negative."

"A double wha?"

"Never mind." Mr. Furnivall frowned severely at Eggy until the young lout removed the parcels and himself from the counter and headed for the back of the store, then returned his attention to Prudence. "Please accept my apologies for his rudeness. At the moment, I have no one else to make deliveries."

"That's quite all right, Mr. Furnivall."

The bookseller sighed. "He is the son of an old friend of mine or I would not have taken him on. He was sacked from his former position—well, perhaps that is not a story your lovely ears should hear, Miss Reese."

She blushed, having never thought of her ears as

lovely or having thought of them at all, in fact. Ears were ears.

"Thank you for your patronage of my humble shop, my dear. And do give my regards to Lady Agatha."

Humble? There were thousands upon thousands of books crowding his shelves. She felt intimidated, but also very glad she had come in. "You seem to have everything, Mr. Furnivall."

Miss Sparks appeared again, a gray cloud against the sunny yellow of her employer's waistcoat, and began a practiced drone. "We stock every title under the sun. Something for everyone."

Prudence nodded.

"We sell almanacs, chapbooks, abecedaria, natural histories and works of science, theoretical and practical," Miss Sparks continued. "Everything for the growing mind and the curious amateur. We also print pamphlets, polemics, and parliamentary reports. And advertising cards for respectable businesses—none of your houses of ill-repute."

Mr. Furnivall interrupted her gently. "I am sure a young lady like Miss Reese knows nothing about such establishments. Thank you, Miss Sparks."

The odd little woman nodded and wandered off down one of the aisles.

"I do apologize, Miss Reese. She says the strangest things sometimes. But her extraordinary memory is useful in my business."

Prudence nodded quickly. "Quite all right. Before I forget—do you stock magazines as well? I might indulge in some light reading this afternoon."

"I not only stock them, I publish one of my own: the *Buckingham Bee*. It is subscribed to by many persons of quality." He gave her a bashful look. "I myself am a writer in a small way, you know. I pen a weekly column for the *Bee* on the subject of politics."

"Really?" Prudence inquired politely, though she could not imagine anything more dull.

He pulled out a copy of the *Bee* from under the counter and flipped through the pages to find his column. "There. The Scourge of Whitehall is my nom de plume."

It was difficult to imagine this gentle old man with the mild blue eyes as the scourge of anything.

"Fancy that. You must get a great deal of mail."

His eyes twinkled. "Sacks, but not as much as Mrs. Motherwit."

"Who?"

He flipped to another page and read aloud. "'Words of Wisdom for the Passionate, the Lovelorn, and the Hopelessly Confused. Mrs. Motherwit answers Selected Questions from Genuine Correspondence. All Replies in the Strictest Confidence.'" He handed it to her.

Prudence examined the engraved portrait that headed the column. It showed an apple-cheeked grandmother in a mobcap and spectacles, with double chins and a descending bosom. "Oh, yes. Our cook mentioned it once. Mrs. Dawkins reads all the papers and she sets particular store by Mrs. Motherwit's advice."

The bookseller looked pleased enough. "The column is all the rage among every social class, Miss Reese. It is now printed in five newspapers but I own the rights to it. Did you know the circulation of the *Bee* more than doubled in the weeks when it first appeared?"

"I see. But is she a real person?"

Mr. Furnivall nodded. "Mrs. Motherwit is my own invention but the writer is a young woman, the devoted mother of two little girls. Her husband—well, went up the Amazon and left no forwarding address—and she was forced to earn her living by her pen."

Prudence nodded. Precisely what she hoped to do. Fortunately, she had a roof over her head and no children. The difficulties that many women experienced through no fault of their own but that of loving the wrong man were truly appalling.

"Alas," Mr. Furnivall continued, "after three years she has saved enough money to open a coffee house. I am looking for a replacement."

"Perhaps I—" Prudence thought over her list of friends and reminded herself that she had none in London. "No, I cannot think of anyone."

"Ah, well." Mr. Furnivall smiled wearily. "Then I must do double duty."

"Oh, dear." Prudence gave him a sympathetic look.

He studied her for a long moment in return. "You are young, Miss Reese, but Lady Agatha says that you are a highly intelligent girl. Perhaps you would like to try writing the column."

"Oh! Certainly not. I know nothing of the world, since I have not made my debut, and I am but a few years from the schoolroom. What could I say to the lovelorn?"

Mr. Furnivall took a pair of spectacles from under the counter and put them on. He peered at her closely. "Have you a kind heart?"

"Ye-es," she stammered. How could she say no to such a question without sounding cold and cruel?

"Well, then. A kind heart and a lively mind are all you need. You would pick it up quite quickly."

The hope in his eyes was distressing. He must be absolutely desperate. Unless—for a moment, literary vanity reared its ugly head—he had somehow sensed her genius.

She wished passionately that she could sense it as well.

"Just look over some of the letters that have come in this week. Pen a few sentences in response. There is not much to it."

"I would have to think about it, Mr. Furnivall," she said firmly. "How many letters does Mrs. Motherwit receive?"

"Ah—it varies."

She hesitated. If she planned to write a romantic novel, reading the communications of real-life lovers might be deeply inspiring—or deeply depressing. There was no way to tell.

Shush-shush. Shush-shush. Miss Sparks appeared at the end of an aisle, dragging a large sack and holding a letter in her hand.

"Today's inquiries to Mrs. Motherwit, in care of the *Buckingham Bee*," she announced in a toneless voice. "I counted three hundred and sixteen. Two are missing sealing wax and one was addressed incorrectly." She held up the one in her hand. "To Mrs. Muggersnit, in care of the *Buckington Bug*."

Mr. Furnivall smiled sadly. "Such is fame. It got here anyway."

"What shall I do with these?"

He sighed. "Put them with the others." He gestured to an enormous basket that was close to overflowing with similar missives. "A cornucopia of correspondence, as you can see, Miss Reese."

They watched Miss Sparks upend the sack and

pour out its contents, then wander away, dragging the empty sack behind her.

Mr. Furnivall gave Prudence a canny look and she shifted uncomfortably on her feet. "Are you quite sure you would not like to try, Miss Reese? You may pick the ones you deem most edifying or amusing, as we cannot answer them all, of course. It is not difficult and it pays well for newspaper work."

She took a deep breath, ready to say no.

"Payment in advance," the bookseller said hastily.

Ah. That sounded more enticing. Perhaps she could cover the costs of her damned debut and get it over with—or flee the country and skip it entirely, she thought. She favored Mr. Furnivall with a demure smile, not wishing to seem too eager. "I see. How much?"

Much to her surprise, he named a sum that would enable her to repay Lady Agatha for every expense of Prudence's stay thus far, including the desk.

Suddenly, reading sacks and sacks of letters seemed like a very attractive way to pass the time. If young Eggy were to deliver them as well, she could begin today. But where to hide them all?

Perhaps Mrs. Dawkins could be persuaded to store them next to the sacks of potatoes and turnips. Lady Agatha almost never entered the kitchen and would want nothing to do with such plebian vegetables in any case.

If the letters were delivered within the hour, Prudence could retrieve them later, when Lady Agatha was out and about. The old lady planned to attend a meeting of a Distinguished Society for the Preservation of Something That Needed Preserving—Prudence could not remember exactly what, but she knew Lady Agatha would not be at home.

"Well, Miss Reese?"

She started, suddenly aware that Mr. Furnivall was waiting for an answer. "Why—yes. I accept your offer. Ah—my advance?"

Mr. Furnivall opened his cash box with an air of regret, as slowly as possible. Perhaps well-brought-up young ladies were not supposed to ask for money, Prudence mused. But he had said payment in advance, so she was only asking for what was rightfully hers.

His eyes widened in astonishment as he poked about in the cash box's compartments. She heard the rattle of a few coins, but only a few.

"Oh dear," he said earnestly. "You have caught me short. I will have to give you your advance later, Miss Reese. But if you would be so good as to write a few replies in the meantime, I would be much obliged."

She scowled at him rather fiercely. The mild-mannered old man was a sly fox when he wanted to be. He gave her the kindest of smiles in return.

"Very well. But you must have Eggy deliver them to the kitchen door before twelve o'clock. Our cook, Mrs. Dawkins, will take over from there. What should I do with the ones I deem unsuitable for the column?"

"Burn them," he said simply. "We cannot keep them if we are to protect the privacy of our correspondents and we do not promise to answer all that we receive. Do read the disclaimer." He picked up the opened *Bee* and pointed to the bottom of Mrs. Motherwit's column.

She peered at it. "The print is excruciatingly fine."

"Of course, Miss Reese. Long words in tiny type seem legal and official."

She nodded, feeling a faint stirring of doubt

about what she was getting into. "Give me a week. I will need at least that long to look through the letters you send. And on second thought, do not send too many."

"Done!" Mr. Furnivall looked extremely happy.

Chapter Ten

Swearing Mrs. Dawkins to secrecy was not difficult. The cook was delighted to hear that Prudence was to be the next Mrs. Motherwit. Mrs. Dawkins was an avid reader of the weekly column, which she passed along to Broderick, who read snippets of it aloud to the interested servants every day.

"But you cannot tell him of this, Mrs. Dawkins," Prudence said.

"I would never tell anyone, miss. Broderick is in the dining room polishing the silver at the moment and admiring his reflection in the spoons. Very vain, he is." The cook smiled broadly. "But our Cathy seems to fancy 'im, or so he says."

Prudence smiled in return. "Well, he is tall and dashing, I suppose."

"Now where is the young lad with the odd name? I heard the clock strike twelve."

A vigorous knock upon the side door answered the cook's question. She left the kitchen to open it and Prudence lingered there, not wanting Eggy to see her but reluctant to leave Mrs. Dawkins to deal with the shopkeeper's boy by herself.

They returned together. Eggy dropped an enormous sack containing what must have been a week's worth of letters in the middle of the kitchen floor, then put the parcel of books upon the table. He looked eagerly about Mrs. Dawkins's spotless domain, where everything was put away in its proper place.

The lad touched a finger to a bright copper bowl and received a slap on the wrist from her less than a second later. "Ow!"

"Ow yerself! Don't touch! I have just polished that there bowl."

"I meant no 'arm!" Egbert whined, rubbing his wrist.

The cook put her hands on her hips and glared at him. "I won't argue with a person named Eggy. 'Tis beneath me dignity."

"Me real name is Egbert. Egbert Weems. Me mum thought it sounded very grand," he whined again. He seemed to take no notice of Prudence, who scarcely knew what to make of this admission.

"Well, Egbert Weems, ye have come and now ye must go," the cook said firmly.

Eggy took note of Prudence at last. "So ye're to be Mrs. Motherwit? What a dreadful lot of letters to read. Ye'll be up all night, Miss Reese."

His familiar remark unsettled her. How much did he know?

"Did Mr. Furnivall tell you that?" Her tone was stern.

"Naow, miss," he said cheekily. "I opened the sack and looked in. I was curious, like. But I didn't open the parcel of books. It was wrapped too tight."

"Curiosity killed the cat, young Eggy," Mrs. Dawkins said as she pulled Marmalady onto her lap.

If only Mrs. Dawkins and the bookseller knew, the secret might be kept. But this lad, who went hither and thither all over London on a thousand errands for his employer, seemed talkative by nature and only too willing to poke his nose into matters that did not concern him.

She had only herself to blame for asking Mr. Furnivall to send Eggy to her home. Had she a coin to bribe the shop lad with? Ought she to do so?

She chided herself for being ten times a fool. "Wait here, please." She took the stairs two at a time to reach her room and was breathless when she got there.

Surely there was a shilling or two in her reticule—if she could find it. She did and there was. She ran downstairs again to see Eggy ignoring Mrs. Dawkins, who patted Marmalady while she waited and kept a careful eye on her copper bowls.

"Here," said Prudence, putting the coin into the lad's hand. "Thank you for bringing the letters so quickly. And please—I must be assured of your discretion."

He nodded. "If I knew what that was, you would be assured of it right quick, miss."

"You must not talk of this to anyone. Promise me."

Eggy smirked at her. "Oh, no. Never. Not me." He tipped his cap in a jaunty way, and went out the way he had come, whistling a jaunty air.

"Miss Reese—what 'ave you done? That young man has a shifty look about 'im, I saw it right off. Not to be trusted, not for a minute. He will rob us of our waluables."

"What?" Prudence asked distractedly.

"Waluables, miss. Them things as what we walue." The cook cast a meaningful look at her copper pots and bowls.

"You may be right, Mrs. Dawkins. Certainly I will

have to buy his continued silence," Prudence said with a sigh. "That is clear enough. If Mr. Furnivall will give me my money—oh, I must start reading."

The cook nodded. "We shall 'oist the sack upstairs together. I cannot do it alone, begging yer pardon, miss."

"Of course not. Mrs. Dawkins, I am very grateful for the assistance you have offered already—and I shall ask Mr. Furnivall not to send so many next time. In fact, perhaps it would be better if I read them at the store."

"Whatever you think is best, Miss Reese. But my lips are sealed. No secret of yours shall escape them."

"I know. And I thank you."

Mrs. Dawkins rose and took one side of the burlap bag and Prudence took the other. They went up quickly, letting the sack bump over the stairs in their haste, and gained the safety of the upper landing, where they rested for a moment.

It was a good thing that the maids were out of the house upon various errands and the footmen were accompanying Lady Agatha to the preservation meeting. As for the others—Lord Alwyn's valet, who he called Disappearing Joseph, and the little page, whose name she always forgot—perhaps they were sleeping. But in any case, Prudence and Mrs. Dawkins had been quick enough to avoid all notice.

The plump cook mopped her brow with a corner of her voluminous apron. "'Tis 'eavy, miss. People 'ave so many problems. 'Owever will ye answer them all?"

"I am to pick only the most interesting problems, Mrs. Dawkins."

The cook thought it over. "Ye might want to sort 'em out to start, like I do with the taties and turnips."

"An excellent idea. Thank you for suggesting it, Mrs. Dawkins."

They heard the front door open and quickly dragged the bag into Prudence's room, stuffing it under the bed. This unusual activity attracted the attention of two of Marmalady's growing kittens, ever on the alert for mischief of all sorts.

The striped kitten pounced on the sack and clawed it fiercely, to no avail. Mrs. Dawkins picked him up and held him to her comfortable bosom. "There, there, my pet. Come with me to the kitchen and we shall see about a dish of cream. A small one, mind ye."

Prudence plucked another kitten from the sack and handed it to Mrs. Dawkins as well. The cook settled her precious cargo and sailed out the door, looking below to see if the coast was clear. It was not.

"Hallo, Lord Alwyn!" Prudence heard her say loudly. "And what brings ye home in the middle of the day?"

Prudence kicked the sack of letters well out of sight under her bed and straightened the covers.

"I was hungry—and the pieman puts too much onion in his goods these days. Is there roast beef left from last night, Mrs. Dawkins?"

"Indeed there is, sir," the cook said heartily. "Come with me. If ye could 'old this 'ere kitten, I would be much obliged."

Prudence heard him laugh.

"I have just removed his brother from the draperies in the hall below. He seemed most interested in the fringe."

"They are playful, sir. 'Tis fortunate that Lady Agatha buys only the best. An 'eavy brocade don't show the marks of their claws."

Prudence stifled a giggle. So long as Lady Agatha did not know that the kittens were climbing her expensive draperies, there was no harm done. Lord Alwyn and the cook proceeded downstairs. Prudence closed her door quietly.

She might as well begin to read. Most likely Mrs. Dawkins would distract Lord Alwyn with a delicious lunch of cold roast beef and her own good bread and let him plunder the remains of the jam tart, as well.

Kneeling, she withdrew the sack, reached within, and picked a few letters at random, opening the first with a fingernail.

Dear Mrs. Motherwit . . .

Prudence felt a glow of pride and read on.

Them as What I Mentioned in my First Letter to You did not read the Column as what You wrote in Return, though I left it open to that Page upon the Teatray, in Hopes of Them as What I Mentioned Taking a Hint. It seems that Things of a Personal Nature have become Publick Knowledge since People Talk, just as You Yourself said would Happen. And so I find Myself in a Curious Quandary from which there is no Ready Escape, though my Person is not Endangered—only My Reputation, such as it is. Now what?

Yours Very Truly,

Bewildered

Prudence sighed. Without the first letter to go by, she could not answer this cryptic missive. The language was too vague for her even to venture a guess at the "Curious Quandary." Clearly, this letter fell into the category of Hopelessly Confused, and the subcategory, Fond of Capital Letters.

Well, she would not worry about it, as the writer was in no danger. She set it aside and opened another.

Dear Mrs. Motherwit,

My husband, a military historian of some renown, will not part with a lifesize waxwork of his dead uncle, a general. How and where he obtained this object—or the uniform and tricorne hat it wears—I do not know. Alas, my husband often discusses famous battles and strategy with it, but he rarely talks to me. What should I do?

Fretful on Fenwick Street.

Prudence thought for a full minute before picking up a stubby pencil and scribbling her reply in the margin.

Dear Fretful,

Keep the waxwork general away from heat and charge admission. Your husband is able to amuse himself, which is a blessing indeed. Many men cannot. What if you had to listen to his talk of yesteryear's battles? You would perish of boredom in a day.

She set it aside in the Lovelorn pile and opened an envelope made of lavender paper. Perhaps this missive would be more romantic.

Dear Mrs. Motherwit,

I cherish a secret tendresse for Signor Suaverino (not his real name, you understand), an Italian count of ancient lineage who is pledged to another. His fiancée is very rich but very plain. Signor Suaverino says that though I am very poor, I am very beautiful, as beautiful as the stars above, and that he wants both of us. But I want only him. What should I do?

Yours sincerely, So In Love With Suaverino

P.S. My brother says that my wayward heart will be my ruination and has promised to horsewhip the so-called signor, whom he calls an impostor and seducer of innocents, or words to that effect. He also says that there are other fish in the sea, etc.

Prudence picked up her pencil again. The writer was romantic, indeed, but also a fool.

Dear So In Love,
Your brother is right. Advise Signor Suaverino of his
comments and invite his fiancée for tea. You can comfort
each other when the signor disappears—and he will.

There. That was easy enough. She tossed the
lavender letter into the Passionate pile and opened
more letters, sorting them quickly.

After several hours, she could only marvel at the infinite capacity of the human heart for self-delusion.
Women, men, the young and the old—all seemed to
think that true love was the answer to all their problems or the cause of all their problems.

Most young women hoped to marry, but the letters from older women proved to Prudence how
often marriages begun in tender hope deteriorated
into daily prizefights.

The letters were not the stuff of which romances
were made, certainly. Well, then—she would be
Mrs. Motherwit for the money and never mind the
inspiration.

A familiar voice interrupted her thoughts.

"Proooo-dence!"

She looked up, setting the envelope in her hand
aside. Lady Agatha was coming upstairs by the
sound of it, though not quickly. What on earth was
Prudence to do with the piles of letters before the
old lady arrived at her door?

She stuffed them back into the sack and strug-
gled to her feet, which had grown slightly numb
from sitting so long upon the floor. Prudence went
out upon the landing, shutting the door to her
bedchamber behind her.

"My dear Lady Agatha! Did you enjoy your meeting? Was everything preserved to your satisfaction?"

Lady Agatha wheezed. "Yes to all questions. And when I change into something more comfortable, perhaps we shall resume our efforts on behalf of the library. Cathy has done as much as she can."

"She is a treasure," Prudence said warmly.

"Indeed she is. By the way, I stopped by the library. Did you know that it is close to complete?"

Prudence gave a guilty start. She did not want to mention her occasional trips to the roof to check upon its progress. Lady Agatha might think that she was checking upon Lord Alwyn as well. "I thought it might be—but I was not sure."

Lady Agatha patted her hand. "There, there. You have been busy writing. And Cathy has been a great help to me since you began your great work. She learns quickly and can sort books by alphabet and by subject."

"Ah—I have not been writing today," Prudence said. Which was true enough. Her hasty replies to Mrs. Motherwit's correspondents did not count.

The old lady raised an inquiring eyebrow.

"I went to Mr. Furnivall's shop and bought an armful of books instead. For research, you see. I must learn more about the world before I can write a novel that would interest sophisticated readers."

Lady Agatha shook her head. "I am not so sure of that. True goodness is much more rare. We do not need to know everything to have valid opinions, my dear. I try to avoid sordid facts myself."

"Oh." This statement seemed like the height of folly to Prudence, but she would rather not argue the point, especially since a bulging sack of sordid facts was now hidden under her bed.

"No, we must keep our minds on higher things and higher thoughts. Have you ever read Bishop Applegate's *Moral Discourses*, my dear? We never did find my copy."

Prudence blushed. Though she now owned two copies, she still had not read a word of it. "Um—no."

"I see," said Lady Agatha, a little sadly. "Did I mention that I plan to invite him and Reverend Ponsonby to dinner soon? But I cannot set the date until I have discussed the menu with Mrs. Dawkins. I gave her several cookery books but she gave me a thoroughly insulted look in return."

"Oh, yes," Prudence said. "You did mention it— I think you did. Oh, dear, what shall I wear?" Both clerics were famous for their unfavorable opinions of female character. Perhaps she should don sackcloth and ashes, or the latest in hair shirts, and a becomingly abject expression.

"It does not matter," Lady Agatha said affably. "Think of it, Prudence! Two renowned churchmen at our table, grappling with the great questions of our day."

"Grappling? Oh, my."

"We shall be treated to learned discussion upon many subjects, my dear."

"And what would those be?" Not that Prudence really wanted to know.

The old lady airily waved a hand. "The usual. The problems of the poor, to start."

"Deserving or undeserving?" Prudence asked pertly.

"Both, I should think. What else?" Lady Agatha put a finger to her chin while she pondered her own question. "The bishop will discuss moral decay, social disintegration, political unrest, evil influences, and so forth."

"Is that all?" Prudence thought there could not possibly be more—but there was.

"Oh, and foreign vices."

"What? Which ones?"

"There are so many," the old lady said fretfully. "The Viennese waltz, for one. It makes young women quite dizzy, and they are easily taken advantage of in that blissful state."

Never having waltzed with anyone but the aged and extremely short dancing master from the town near her birthplace, Prudence could not agree or disagree.

"What else?" Lady Agatha continued. "Oh, French food, revealing fashions, the needless importation of lapdogs—there is no subject too trivial for Reverend Ponsonby. He hopes to keep the bloodlines of our sturdy English breeds pure but dogs will be dogs, you know."

"Yes, Lady Agatha."

"What else? How could I forget: the scandal-mongering penny press! The bishop held forth last Sunday upon the shockingly low standards of our London journalists."

It occurred to Prudence that she was now of this tribe. Would the kindly guise of Mrs. Motherwit provoke the bishop's righteous wrath? Surely not. But Prudence certainly would not mention her temporary employment in this field. "Dear me. They shall be talking throughout dinner."

Lady Agatha beamed. "From the soup to the savories. I am looking forward to it."

"And I as well," Prudence said politely.

"Alwyn will be there. He has been asking most

particularly after you, Prudence. It seems that you are not home when he is, and vice versa." Lady Agatha peered closely at Prudence, who said nothing. "Dear boy. He regrets being away so much lately, but he said he would not miss such a dinner for the world."

Prudence wondered why. He had made his disdain for these two clergymen quite clear. Perhaps he intended to debate various points of theology, just for the fun of it. But Lord Alwyn had little interest in the subject, as far as she knew.

Perhaps he was showing up merely to please his mother. Certainly it had nothing to do with her, Prudence thought, feeling a little sad.

Her eyes widened and she stifled a little gasp. Surely he would not tease Bishop Applegate about the drawings she had found—Lord Alwyn had kept the first five, of that Prudence was fairly sure. He had not returned them to her, in any case.

She would not tell him that she now possessed the next in the series, again found quite by chance. *By chance.* It suddenly occurred to her that Lord Alwyn could not have put the five new drawings she now had in the copy of *Moral Discourses* from Mr. Furnivall's bookshop. Lord Alwyn would have had no way of knowing that she was there today, and so would not have hidden them for her benefit. Therefore, he had probably not hidden the first ones, either.

Oh, dear. He might not be guilty after all. The thought made her blush, for she had boldly accused him of doing just that. If only he had looked more innocent.

But he could not help that, she supposed. He was a man of the world, who made no secret of his superior experience. He had a reputation as a rake, though precisely why was something that had never been made clear to her. Yet she had believed him capable of such mischief and worse.

Now she did not know what to think.

The day was fine, and Lord Alwyn was rather at loose ends. Herrick had all but shooed him away from the library, as his presence was not required at this point in its construction. He wondered where he might go instead and what he might do once he was there.

Perhaps he could call upon Charles. His friend and business partner had not been seen at the site for a few days. Alwyn was bound to find him strolling in St. James Park or somewhere else nearby.

Alwyn had an idea or two for their next project that he hoped to discuss—and he might as well ask a few casual questions on quite another subject: love. Why not? Alwyn reasoned. Charles fancied himself an expert on the matter. He would not mention Miss Reese's name, of course, but speak only in the most general terms.

He had a feeling she was avoiding him. Even for someone who was writing a novel, she spent far too much time in her room. However, he had seen nothing but letters upon her blue desk and those only once—letters she had hastily swept into a drawer when she realized he happened to be walking down the hall that led to their respective bedchambers. Was someone writing to her? More importantly, was she writing back?

Another odd thing: his mama seemed to have forgotten the business of Prudence's debut. According to Disappearing Joseph, his increasingly absent valet, they did not shop or visit dressmakers nor had any mantua-makers or milliners visited the house.

As far as he knew, the girl divided her time between the house and Furnivall's bookshop. Perhaps she was turning into a bluestocking after all, which would be a dreadful waste of feminine charm. He vowed to wait no longer.

He had guessed right. She was at the bookstore.

Prudence had decided, unbeknownst to all, to stop in at Mr. Furnivall's and ask a few questions of the person who knew exactly where everything was at all times. Miss Sparks might very well know something about the naughty drawings in the bishop's virtuous book.

Prudence had come up with a theory, which she explained in detail.

But the odd little woman in gray took some time to think about it. Miss Sparks examined the drawings with an expression of faint disgust, while Prudence turned pink with embarrassment.

At least they were behind a very tall bookcase, where the proprietor could not see them, Prudence thought, looking around.

"Most interesting," said Miss Sparks at last. "You say you found these in *Moral Discourses*? And that it had been placed on the wrong shelf?"

"Yes," Prudence said. "And Eggy was loitering nearby, looking at me in the rudest way. I did not think then that he might have had something to do with it, but it seems the only possibility."

Miss Sparks sighed. "And you mentioned that you

found others in a book of boxes from Mr. Furnivall,
is that correct?"

"Yes. I think that the box was from Mr. Furnivall,
but I cannot be positive. We received thousands of
donations."

She received only a sour smile from Miss Sparks,
who looked again at the drawings. "Eggy packed
those boxes. No doubt he thought it a great joke to
put in something scandalous for you or Lady Agatha
to find. Perhaps he overheard Lady Agatha telling
Mr. Furnivall of your presence in her house."

"That occurred to me," Prudence said. "It seemed
too great a coincidence otherwise. And he must
have prepared the second volume and slipped it
upon the shelf somehow before I saw him do it,
hoping that I would notice a book of sermons upon
the romance shelf."

"Eggy used to work for a bookbinder. He was
sacked for a similar prank, you know, or so Mr. Furnivall gave me to understand."

"Oh," said Prudence, not surprised.

"He bound drinking songs into a hymnbook. But
this time—if he did put these pictures into the
bishop's book—is rather worse. The question remains as to where he got them."

Prudence raised an eloquent eyebrow, not wanting to suggest theft. She had only wanted to find
out more, and though she did not like Eggy, she
had no wish to see him transported for his youthful
folly.

Miss Sparks continued. "Mr. Furnivall hired him
out of duty but he told me to keep an eye on the
boy." She sighed. "But I have been too busy. And
Eggy got up to his tricks again, it seems. My apologies,
Miss Reese."

"It is not your fault," Prudence hastened to assure her.

Miss Sparks handed the drawings back to Prudence. "I will have to talk to Mr. Furnivall."

Prudence put a hand upon the gray woman's arm. "Please do not, Miss Sparks. We have no proof of Eggy's wrongdoing, only conjecture. And the matter is not as important as all that."

The shop assistant shrugged. "As you wish."

Perhaps Miss Sparks did not wish Mr. Furnivall to think she had been less than punctilious. As far as Prudence was concerned, the matter was now resolved. She now knew enough to believe that Lord Alwyn had not placed the drawings in either book.

Alwyn found Charles the way he always did: by looking for the prettiest woman in the park. If Charles did not already have the latest Incomparable on his arm, he would be somewhere near her, attempting to catch her eye and flattering her with astonishing compliments.

It was all good sport. The participants in the great and endless flirtations of late spring in London knew the rules, and most obeyed them. Of course, love had very little to do with it.

Ah—there he was. Alwyn looked on as a popular beauty fixed Charles with a haughty stare and sauntered away with her companion.

"Is there something in your eye, Sudbury?" Alwyn inquired.

"What?" Charles turned. "Oh, it is you! No, I was winking. I am out of practice. She seemed not in the least impressed."

"Do you never grow tired of these amorous antics, my friend?"

"No. Never."

They strolled on, nodding to acquaintances and exchanging polite greetings with friends now and then.

"So what brings you out on this beautiful day, Alwyn? You never did say."

"No, I did not."

"But there is a purpose for everything you do. And I must know it—gad, what a magnificent female!" He made an extravagant bow to another promenading beauty and nearly fell into a fishpond. Alwyn helped him right himself.

"Do be careful, Charles. You will be wearing a lily pad for a hat and a goldfish for an earring if you trip over your feet every time you see a pretty woman."

"Ah, what a man must do for love," Charles said cheerfully.

"Well—in fact, that was why I wanted to see you."

"I beg your pardon?" Charles gaped at him. "Are *you* in love?"

"No, no, not at all," Alwyn hastened to assure him. "I merely wanted to ask a few general questions on the subject. Just in case it happens—someday."

"I see." Charles walked more slowly, his hands clasped behind his back. "Then I am at your service. Ask away."

"If a woman who at first seemed interested—"

Charles interrupted. "What woman are you speaking of?"

Alwyn cleared his throat. "If this entirely hypothetical woman seems—somewhat less interested—does that mean that I have offended her in some way?"

"Probably," Charles said. "Women enjoy being offended. They take a peculiar pleasure in that state, in fact. They are deucedly difficult to apologize to."

"Then what should I do?" Alwyn looked quite worried.

"You must apologize for everything in advance."

"But I have done nothing wrong, Charles!"

"It doesn't matter, my friend. You are forgetting how the female mind works. Even if you have done nothing wrong, you eventually will. A shrewd man always says he is sorry first—and then does exactly as he pleases."

Lord Alwyn cast him a doubtful look. "Your logic is hard to follow."

"It works. That's all I know."

"What else should I do?"

"The usual. Praise, flattery, flowers, chocolates. Make her laugh. Do your best to listen to her—women love a good listener—and do not go on and on about your perfect taste and superior education. You can be a dreadful prig at times, Alwyn."

"You are honest to a fault," Alwyn muttered.

"You did ask."

"I have only one more question, Charles—have *you* ever been in love?"

"Of course. Sometimes twice a day. Good morning, my dear!" Charles tipped his hat to another woman, rather less elegant but no less beautiful than the others, who rewarded him with a come-hither look. "I really must be going. Ta-ta, old friend." He slapped Alwyn on the back and followed his true love *du jour* down a shady path.

Chapter Eleven

A few weeks later . . .

Alwyn was taking tea with Mrs. Dawkins at the old pine table in the kitchen amidst the usual clutter of newspapers and cookery books. The largest of these was currently serving as a doorstop. Mrs. Dawkins insisted that she had no need for them, though they had been a gift from Lady Agatha.

He looked about the kitchen, admiring its cream-colored walls and the afternoon light that poured in through the basement window above the sink. Red geraniums, Mrs. Dawkins's favorite flower, stood in a neat row of pots upon the sill, doing as well as might be expected for plants that saw the sun but once a day. The household china was arranged neatly in racks upon the walls and polished pots and pans gleamed by the stove.

He was comfortable in this cozy place and always had been. His mother, ever busy with good causes and eccentric projects, never knew how many hours he had spent in the cook's company.

Mrs. Dawkins was baking and the room was quite warm. Alwyn had taken off his waistcoat the moment he entered and picked a chair that was sturdy enough for him to lean back in and relax.

Now that the library had progressed to a point near completion, he had time to turn his attention to the goings-on at Purcell House once more. He had not stayed in his own apartments for weeks. Of course, there had been the disastrous collapse, the painstaking rebuilding—*hang it,* he thought—Miss Prudence Reese was the real reason he had chosen to stay here.

His man, Joseph, had mentioned in passing that Prudence seemed to be friendly with the cook and Lord Alwyn thought he might glean some information concerning that young lady from Mrs. Dawkins, however inadvertently she might provide it.

If Miss Reese was absorbed in her writing, well and good. If she were a social butterfly he might have reason to be worried, but Prudence was not. Still, he had scarcely caught a glimpse of her lately. She was forever locked away behind the door of her bedroom, or out at the Furnivall bookshop, or otherwise engaged in worthy pursuits. Or so his mother said.

"The tea is excellent, Mrs. Dawkins," he said, finishing his. "Most restorative. Exactly what I needed."

She set down her mug of tea and brushed the crumbs of her toast from the table into her hand. She rose to put these outside on the sill of the basement window, as was her habit. "For the sparrers, sir," she explained. "They do enjoy a taste of good bread."

Lord Alwyn smiled at the plump cook, whose affection for animals and birds was well-known in the family. In fact, she had called him to the kitchen to discuss a matter of extraordinary importance: the kittens.

Marmalady's offspring were big and rumbustious, and the old cat would no longer let them nurse. It was time to give them away, but Mrs. Dawkins insisted that they go to good homes.

He looked down at the orange kitten, which slumbered against his boot. "Shall we keep this one, Mrs. Dawkins?"

"Is it a male or a female?"

He scooped it up with a hand and lifted its tail for a look. "Decidedly male." The sleepy kitten let out an indignant squeal and he handed it to her.

"A Marmaladdie, is it? Oh, that won't do," the cook chuckled. "Can't keep a tomcat in a house. The smell is dreadful."

Alwyn nodded. "I bow to your wisdom in these matters, Mrs. D. Perhaps Herrick might take him. The men have seen rats around the building . . . but then they will leave the remnants of their lunch about."

Mrs. Dawkins cuddled the orange kitten. "Only if they make him a little house of his own. I'll not have Marmalady's children turned out in the cold."

"I am sure that can be arranged." He nodded solemnly. "I will talk to Herrick today. I think my cousin would like the calico. It is a pretty cat, and female. A perfect pet."

"Indeed it is," said Mrs. Dawkins.

"The black-and-whites will go to the tavern owner—and perhaps I shall keep the striped one for sentimental reasons." He picked it up and put it in his lap. "Marmalady took it to the roof and Miss Reese helped with its rescue."

"She seems a very kind girl, sir," Mrs. Dawkins said approvingly. "And lively."

"Yes." Alwyn fell silent.

The cook hummed an old country song and petted the orange kitten in her lap. Lord Alwyn seemed to have something on his mind. He might want to talk—he had confided in her now and then in his boyhood, sometimes confessing to a bit of bad behavior. The trick was to pretend to be thinking about something else entirely.

His youthful sins had been of the most minor kind, such as putting frogs where frogs should not be—once, in his mother's big jewelry box. The poor little creature leaped forth to freedom when Lady Agatha opened the lid, landing upon her bosom. Her shriek brought everyone running, including the gleeful Master Alwyn.

The memory made Mrs. Dawkins smile fondly at him.

"She does seem so," Lord Alwyn mused.

"Who?" said the cook, pretending to have forgotten what they were talking about.

"Miss Reese. She seems very kind."

"She is a lovely girl, sir. Full of spirit."

"Do you know that she hopes to write a book?"

"She is at it for hours each day, sir. I have strict instructions to leave the tea tray outside her door when she is working." Mrs. Dawkins did not quite meet his gaze, remembering her vow to keep Miss Reese's secret and tell no one that the girl was writing Mrs. Motherwit's column.

"And then there are letters—she seems to write a great many," he said thoughtfully.

"I imagine she has many friends, sir. No doubt she tells them every little thing, as girls will do."

The cook had no idea what Prudence told her friends, but she wished to steer Lord Alwyn away from the dangerous subject of letters.

"No doubt. She is very busy."

"Yes, sir. She is at that." Mrs. Dawkins knew that the poppet had set aside the book she'd hoped to write and seemed quite happy to have done so.

Prudence had declared that she was learning more about human nature and the human heart than she had imagined possible—and that it would take a broad understanding of such matters to write a novel.

In any case, the girl only wanted to earn some money and have a bit of fun. Surely there was no harm in that. Much of what she made went to buy books on every subject under the sun, including philosophy and medicine. Mrs. Dawkins was most impressed by these tomes, which Eggy delivered, though she no longer allowed the lad inside her kitchen.

Prudence was acquiring an education, and all on her own, too.

But there was no telling what a man might think of such an endeavor. If Lord Alwyn fancied Miss Reese, as he seemed to, Mrs. Dawkins had all the more reason to keep her mouth shut.

"Mrs. Dawkins, may I ask you a hypothetical question?"

The plump cook nodded. What a hypothetical question was, she did not know, but she was about to find out. Lord Alwyn settled the striped kitten more comfortably in his lap and leaned forward, putting his elbows upon the pine table and propping his chin in his hands.

At the moment, he looked all of ten years old, for

all that he was so dark and dashing. "Ye may ask me any question at all, sir."

"If a man is in love, how does he know it?"

Mrs. Dawkins took a deep breath. So it was not mere fancy but love. She would have to consider her answer quite carefully.

"Oh—well, he can think of nothing save his sweetheart, I s'pose."

"Men think about women all the time. But love must be different somehow."

"Why are ye asking me, sir?"

Alwyn shrugged. "Why not? Were you not married once?"

Mrs. Dawkins took a little while to reply. "Yes, when I was a young lass. But before I came to London . . . Mr. Dawkins was transported to Australia for poaching and he never came back. We had no children, so it did not matter." She stroked the soft fur of the kitten in her lap absentmindedly.

"My dear Mrs. Dawkins, forgive me. I did not mean to bring up painful memories."

"I think it were most painful for the kangaroos he met, sir. He sent me a letter saying as what he shot several, just for fun. That were the last I heard of him and that were years ago. No, I don't miss 'im."

Perhaps the best thing to do under the circumstances was to say no more, Lord Alwyn mused. He had always understood in a vague sort of way that Mrs. Dawkins was a widow, but the particulars had never been explained to him.

Indeed, perhaps his mother had known nothing of Mrs. Dawkins's past. He thought of the cook's maternal devotion to him over the years and felt even more ashamed of his tactlessness.

"Mrs. Dawkins, allow me to make amends."

"That was long ago . . . and ye meant no harm, I'm sure."

"Well, no, of course not—but I could arrange it so you had a full day off each week."

The cook gave him a dubious look. "I have my half-Sundays, sir."

"Hm. But my mother insists that you attend Reverend Ponsonby's church, is that right?"

Mrs. Dawkins nodded. She had recently been apprised of some interesting information concerning Ponsonby, which she could not share with Lord Alwyn or her mistress. Still, she would be delighted not to have to listen to the old hypocrite.

"Then you shall have a full Sunday, with no Ponsonby. How would that be?"

"I should like that very much, sir," said Mrs. Dawkins. "If you would make the arrangement with milady, I would be eternally grateful."

Lord Alwyn grinned at her. "Will it guarantee me an eternal supply of this good bread?"

"Certainly. I have been teaching Cathy how to bake, you know. She is eager to learn and quick about her work. I think that your mother has plans for her."

"Oh dear," sighed Lord Alwyn. "Life gets a little too interesting when my mother starts making plans. Do you know, I sometimes wonder whether she means to throw me together with Miss Reese . . . " He trailed off. Though he would trust Mrs. Dawkins to keep his every secret, as she always had, perhaps he ought not to mention this one.

He reminded himself that he was not sure of his feelings for that charming young lady, and that he wished to wait, and so forth. Yet he quailed under the cook's steady gaze. He had said too much again. Mrs. Dawkins seemed positively fascinated by his casual remark.

If there were the least hint of a budding romance, women were instantly aflutter, he thought, feeling a little panicked. He attempted a hearty laugh but it sounded false, even to his ears. "I should ask Mrs. Motherwit for advice, I suppose. You follow her column in the *Buckingham Bee*, do you not, Mrs. Dawkins?"

"Well—yes," she said rather slowly. Had he guessed—or been told—that Prudence was writing it? Had her first replies to the Passionate, the Lovelorn, and the Hopelessly Confused already appeared in print?

Mrs. Dawkins had not read the most recent *Bee* and could not be sure. It occurred to her that someone might have talked. That disrespectful Eggy Weems, perhaps, who had been so bold as to manhandle her mixing bowls. The lad was capable of far worse, she suspected. But she said nothing more.

Lord Alwyn noticed somewhat absently that the plump cook's mouth seemed to be clamped into a tight line. Had he offended her again? Surely he was upon safe ground if they discussed a newspaper column of such popularity. Everyone read Mrs. Motherwit.

He rummaged through the papers on the table. "Ah—here is the *Bee*. Perhaps the dear old thing will have something to say on the subject." He opened the paper with a flourish and leafed through its pages.

He read silently for a moment, then laughed aloud. "This one speaks for every fool in love, Mrs. Dawkins."

"Do tell," she said nervously.

"Shall I read it to you?" Without waiting for a reply, he began.

"*Dear Mrs. Motherwit. I am Huncommonly Devoted to a Certain Young Lady who Knows Naught of My Feelings for Her. My situation is Hunfortunate. I see her every day, walking by where I works—but she does not look my way! I have been given to Hunderstand that she makes First-Rate Gingerbread and I sincerely hope to make her my Wife. But how can I make her notice me? Yours Truly, An Invisible Man.* Poor fellow. I know something of how he feels."

"Do you, sir?"

Lord Alwyn looked up. He would not elaborate upon his statement, even to dear Mrs. Dawkins. "Ah—would you like to hear Mrs. Motherwit's reply?"

"Certainly."

"*Dear Invisible. If you know that she makes excellent gingerbread, then you obviously know someone who knows her. Arrange an introduction to the young lady through this person. She undoubtedly wants to get out of the kitchen and away from that hot stove. Take her to Vauxhall or some other pretty place and proceed from there. A few words of advice: do not rush. A budding romance must have time in which to flower!*" He set the paper down. "Excellent advice, is it not, Mrs. Dawkins? Mrs. Dawkins?"

The plump cook's mouth was open and her eyes were wide. She seemed to be looking at something in back of him. Lord Alwyn turned to see—no one at all. The doorway to the kitchen was empty and he heard no sound of footsteps.

"Beggin' yer pardon, sir," she said quickly. "I thought there was a—a mouse."

"Upon my shoulder? I rather doubt it," he replied.

"Oh, I was imagining things. Read me another, do." She would have to keep him talking long enough for Miss Reese, whom she guessed stood pressed to the wall beside the open door, to make her escape.

"Hmph." He picked up the paper again. "*Dear Mrs. Motherwit. I found my husband in flagrante delicto with a female who must remain nameless, though she is widely known—*"

"What is a *flagrante delicto*, Lord Alwyn? Sounds like an Eyetalian word to me. Is it a bed, then?"

"Yes, you might say that," he agreed, and continued, though Mrs. Dawkins was no longer giving him her full attention. She watched Miss Reese tiptoe past the open door behind him, a finger to her lips. Mrs. Dawkins gave Lord Alwyn her full attention when Prudence was safely out of sight.

He went on. "*I demanded that the female return to the squalid street whence she came—and she did, though she wore nothing save her corset and her drawers. My husband threw the covers over his head and refused to leave the bed.*"

"The *flagrante delicto*, you mean," the cook corrected him.

"Yes, Mrs. Dawkins. The writer does not say whether her husband has come out from under the covers, however, and we must assume that this happened weeks ago," he laughed. "Now what would you do in such a situation?"

Mrs. Dawkins looked suitably scandalized, though she knew he was only teasing. "I would go back to my mother, sir."

"What if you had no mother?"

"I would send such a husband back to *his* mother. She would give him what for and it would serve him right."

"Very good, Mrs. Dawkins! And do you know, Mrs. Motherwit agrees with you. That is exactly what she recommends."

The cook smiled nervously. Miss Reese, an innocent if ever there was one, had consulted her on this very letter, though Prudence had not read its every detail aloud as Lord Alwyn seemed about to do. "She is a very clever girl—I mean, a clever woman, sir."

"Pooh. Mrs. Motherwit is imaginary, you may be sure. The column is undoubtedly penned by a Grub Street hack who writes the letters as well as the replies."

Mrs. Dawkins shook her head. "Oh no. It is all as real as real can be. There are more people as what reads it than ever. Even your mother, sir—Lady Agatha always asks for the *Bee* these days. I send it up with her afternoon cuppa."

He shrugged. There was no reason to argue the point.

"Speaking of that, she will be expecting it soon— and you. Did she not tell you?"

"No."

Mrs. Dawkins looked puzzled. Lady Agatha had actually made her way down to the kitchen some hours ago to enlist the cook's help and Cathy's. She had explained that Alwyn and Prudence were both to appear at tea today and that no excuses would be accepted. The old lady had muttered something about a mother's work never being done and left.

"You must dress, sir, and I must put the kettle

on." She rose, moving the kitten from her lap to a cookery book, and bustled about.

Lord Alwyn sighed. "I will be awash in tea, I'm afraid. I dare not tell her that I have already had some with you."

"Miss Reese is to be there as well."

"Really?" Had he struck the right note of casual indifference to that wonderful fact? Alwyn rather doubted it, judging by the wink the cook gave him. "By the way—about the kittens. Shall I take the orange one to Herrick tomorrow?"

"I suppose it is time. At least I may visit it upon occasion."

"Indeed you may, Mrs. Dawkins. You may be sure that he will be treated like royalty, as befits a son of Marmalady, even an illegitimate one."

"How you do go on, sir! I shall thrash Herrick myself if he isn't," she said, laughing.

She got the fire going and filled a huge metal kettle with water, setting it upon the stove to boil. Cathy had left the other tea things in readiness, so there was nothing else to do for the moment. The cook sat down to catch her breath, watching Alwyn collect the kittens so she might cuddle the purring brood in her capacious lap one last time.

"Thank you for the tea, Mrs. Dawkins."

"You are quite welcome, sir." She returned her attention to the kittens. Marmalady looked massively bored with the whole business and not in the least sentimental about their leavetaking, as was natural for the mother of so many.

Alwyn took the stairs from the basement kitchen two at a time, slowing his pace as he came into the hall. He smoothed his hair in the mirror of the chiffomonster, realizing that, although he was tall, he looked even taller in the distorted glass. At last—a reason to like the damned thing. He gave its carved side a pat and then galloped up the stairs to dress for tea.

Chapter Twelve

Having escaped upstairs a half hour previously, Prudence set about the task of burning the letters she had answered and a handful of those she had not. Mrs. Dawkins, her conspirator, had taken care of the rest this morning in the much larger kitchen stove.

Mr. Furnivall had been quite pleased with her first columns, made a few suggestions as to the next, and scraped up her advance at last. She had arranged to select the next letters while at the store, directly from the sacks, so as not to have to contend with so many. Should anyone notice the smell of burning paper, she could not pretend to be suddenly afflicted with pyromania.

Fortunately, the Rumford stove in her room was new and the small fire within it burned cleanly. Prudence fed the letters to the flames one by one, watching each shrivel, blacken, and go up in smoke. Ghostly phrases caught her eye. *Does he love me? She loves another. My mother-in-law interferes. My digestion is troubled. He loves me not—what shall I do? She loves me, but my mother-in-law interferes.*

The sameness of most of the queries made the task of answering—or not answering them—rather routine. Prudence set aside the truly heartbreaking ones to answer privately. She would never publish these.

Not every difficulty could be helped, especially where women and children were concerned, but the least she could do was pen a few lines of heartfelt comfort to the afflicted in body and spirit.

When she was finished, Prudence opened the windows and waved away the traces of smoke. The summer day was breezy, which helped.

Then she sat before a Venetian mirror propped upon a vanity and studied her face, which was flushed. Was it from burning those few letters or from her mad dash up the stairs? She had not expected to see Lord Alwyn in the kitchen, chatting so amiably with the cook.

She had scarcely seen him at all in the last weeks, but as busy with reading as she had been, that was to be expected. She had just finished the difficult books and treated herself to *The Loves of Lady Lascivia* for dessert.

Thinking of his handsomeness made her sigh. He did not even have to turn around for her foolish heart to beat faster—just a glimpse of his dark hair curling over the back of his collar had been enough. He had been leaning back in the kitchen chair, reading aloud to Mrs. Dawkins, with his boot heels set upon the table rail and his legs spread wide under its top.

Reading my column, she thought with a shudder. What if he knew that she was Mrs. Motherwit? Prudence put the idea out of her mind immediately.

She had to think of something else—but she could only think of him. He had not been wearing a waistcoat in the warm kitchen, she noted. The sight of his broad shoulders in the plain linen shirt took her mind back to their evening upon the roof—an event that seemed by now to have happened in a dream.

She supposed that she might have entered the kitchen and spoken to him, but she had felt unaccountably shy. Truth to tell, it had been too long since she had seen him, and she was discomfited to find that an accidental meeting could make her so nervous.

Prudence hoped and prayed she was not in love.

As Mrs. Motherwit, she had learned rather too much about that subject. Certainly everyone seemed to want to be loved and to love somebody in return, but precious few were actually happy with the love they found. Or perhaps people who were happy in love did not have the time to write letters, being busy with more important things like cooing and hugging and kissing.

There had been scarcely any letters on kissing. Judging by her three categories of correspondents, the Passionate already knew all about it and the Lovelorn, sadly, had never even come close. Of course, not even the Hopelessly Confused would ask an old lady, as Mrs. Motherwit supposedly was, how it was done.

And a good thing, too. Prudence did not really know much about the subject. Her one and only kiss had lasted but a fraction of a second, though Lord Alwyn had seemed upon the verge of others once or twice since then. Still, between his library and her book, there had been no further opportunities.

She saw him but rarely. Why did she think about him so often? She rose from the vanity and crossed the room to her bed, flinging herself into the pillows like the heroine of a romantic novel. A few feathers floated up into the afternoon sunlight above her head and she caught one in her hand.

There was a knock upon the door.

"Come in," Prudence said, letting go of the feather. The breeze from the window lifted it away.

Cathy entered almost noiselessly and Prudence sat up.

"I have come to dress your hair, miss. Lady Agatha thought you might want to join her and Lord Alwyn for tea."

Tea? The invitation was unexpected but most welcome. Perhaps her shyness would disappear—and surely pleasant conversation would be better than contemplating the problems of mankind, Prudence thought.

She ran a hand through her tangled locks. "If you can turn this bird's-nest into something more attractive, I should be much obliged." She bounced off the bed and returned to the vanity, where she looked at herself in the mirror. Her hair was a sorry sight indeed.

Cathy picked up a brush and ran it gently through Prudence's wayward curls. "Your hair is very pretty. I would be grateful if mine was not red."

"Why?" The soothing strokes of the brush made Prudence relax.

"The men comment on it, miss. And on other things. I make sure to wear a bonnet when I go out shopping, and a loose dress."

"I understand." Prudence's irritable mood lessened with each stroke of the brush. "That feels very pleasant. You might do this for a living, Cathy."

The maid smiled. "I often dressed my younger sisters' hair when my mother was busy."

"She had a sweet-shop, did she not?"

"Yes, miss. We all helped her make candies and nougats and jelly drops. Even my older brother helped."

"And did he grow up to be a candymaker?"

Cathy continued to brush Prudence's hair. "No, miss. He became a bricklayer. But they set him to mixing the mortar first, and he often thought how much it was like stirring candy."

"You must show me how someday."

Cathy shook her head. "It is harder work than you think. Baking is easier. Mrs. Dawkins has been teaching me to make bread and cakes."

Prudence smiled at her in the mirror. "Well, well. From books to baking. You are learning quite a lot at the Purcell household."

"Yes, miss." Cathy smiled shyly in return. She swept up Prudence's hair into a loose knot and pinned it securely, pulling out a few tendrils to frame her face. "There. Shall I add a little bow or a flower?"

"Oh, my. That looks very pretty. Perhaps nothing more is needed." Prudence admired her reflection, turning this way and that. It would not do to have Lord Alwyn think she was trying to impress him, even if she wanted to do just that.

Cathy had moved to the closet and brought forth a few dresses that Prudence had forgotten about. She rose to inspect them, choosing one of a pale shell-pink. With the maid's assistance, it was not long before she was fully dressed.

And looking rather better than she had for some time, Prudence thought, peeping one last time in the glass. She thanked the maid and went down to tea.

***

Lord Alwyn was waiting upon the first floor landing, in front of a door that was very rarely opened. His dark eyes lit up when he saw Prudence come down the stairs. The bodice of her dress was cut lower than her usual modest frocks. He reminded himself not to look down when he was talking to her. Unless she was looking away, of course.

He bowed ever so slightly when she stood beside him.

"My dear Miss Reese, you do look lovely. Mama said we might await her in the drawing room."

She smiled up at him, positively sparkling. "I have never been into it. I thought that room was set aside for solemn occasions."

"No," he said. "It was simply so cluttered that it was difficult to open the door without Broderick's assistance. Mama has had some of the furniture removed and sent back to Tottenham Court Road from whence it came."

He did not mention that he had been there earlier in the day with the five drawings found in the bishop's book. The dealer in prints and paintings whom Alwyn had consulted thought they were the work of Boucher, perhaps studies for paintings that had not been completed. As to their value, the man could not say. He had offered to try and find the remaining ten in the series, though he could make no promises on that score. The dealer had agreed that they were charming indeed.

But nothing was so charming as Miss Reese, Alwyn thought. He opened the door for her and let her enter first.

The drawing room was hung with opulent silks in a riot of colors, and the theme seemed to be floral.

Immense blossoms and stylized leaves covered the walls and the upholstery, and the very furniture seemed to twist and twine.

"Hm," he said, looking about. "She did not remove as much as I hoped. This is a jungle, not a drawing room."

Prudence laughed. "I rather like the effect. One could be lost in here for days, Lord Alwyn."

"Indeed. And here comes enough food for an army of explorers and a rescue party."

His mother bustled in, followed by Broderick, who shouldered an ebony tea tray of imperial dimensions. Upon it were the silver tea service, several porcelain teacups, and a small mountain of cakes, muffins, and scones upon a silver platter.

"What were you saying about explorers, Alwyn?"

"Nothing, Mama."

She settled herself in a throne carved with foliage and rested her slippers on a tree-trunk footstool. "Observe the pastries! Mrs. Dawkins is teaching Cathy to bake. Has she not performed wonders, Broderick?"

The butler, who had not forgiven the maid for ignoring his virile strength, nodded curtly. "Yes, m'am." He set the tray down upon the only clear surface in the room and stalked out.

"Well, well. Here we all are, together at last," said Lady Agatha affably. "Tea?"

She poured, the platter was passed around, and a happy fuss was made over the perfection of the cakes.

"You are in good spirits, Mama," said Lord Alwyn. "It is a pleasure to see you so cheerful."

"I am always cheerful, Alwyn. It is you who are irritable now and then. But now that the library is almost finished, you can rejoin the human race and partake of ordinary pleasures. Scone?"

She picked one up with the tongs and thrust it at him.

Alwyn managed a smile, though he had already consumed three at Mrs. Dawkins's table. "Certainly, Mama. Thank you."

Lady Agatha put it upon the saucer that held his teacup, bumping the cup and spilling the tea upon the carpet. Though its bizarre design rendered the stain invisible, the old lady seemed upset.

"Oh, dear. Where is Broderick? Where is Cathy? Where is—oh, pray excuse me!" Before Alwyn or Prudence could stop her, she rose from her throne and went in search of a servant.

"Do you suppose she intends to leave us alone?" asked Lord Alwyn, amused. So his mama did intend to throw them together. He had suspected as much. His long hours at the building site had only temporarily thwarted such obvious matchmaking, it seemed.

"I have no idea," said Prudence. If that was the old lady's intention, it would not be at all polite to speculate upon it.

They fell silent. No doubt, Lady Agatha would return within moments—perhaps that was why neither of them could think of a word to say.

Prudence toyed with the petals of the rose in the bouquet upon the tea tray and looked self-consciously about the room. The draperies—most interesting. The wallpaper—likewise. The rug— an object of extreme fascination. The sound of Alwyn clearing his throat made her look up at last.

"I suppose you have been busy writing your book."

"Yes," said Prudence demurely. "The process of literary creation is a consuming one."

"And how goes it?"

"What?"

"The book," Alwyn said. "What else?"

She thought of the sacks of letters under her bed and felt a little guilty. Should she explain that she had run out of inspiration at the first sight of a piece of blank paper and locked the untouched ream in her desk? No. Should she tell him that she was the new Mrs. Motherwit? Again, no. She had only written a few columns, though she had read scores of letters and there were scores more awaiting her attention.

"It is going very well. The twists and turns of the plot are too complex to explain, however."

"I am sure it will be a great success. Is it a romance?"

"Ah—it might be."

"Then put in our encounter upon the roof. That was a memorable evening. And do you know, Mama never asked me afterwards what I was doing in your room in my drawers."

"Well, well." She could think of nothing intelligent to say to that.

"You could pen a cracking good romance." He smiled affably, per Charles's instructions. What had his friend recommended? Praise, flattery, flowers—there were already too many in this room—chocolates. There were no chocolates. But he could make up for that later. At the moment he was doing his best not to be a prig.

Prudence looked at him suspiciously. "You do not have a high opinion of romances. Why do you think I should write one?"

He did not reply immediately. He seemed to be thinking.

Which was exactly what he was doing. *Because you inspire romantic feelings in me, Miss Reese. Because with your hair in such pretty disarray, you look like the heroine of a romantic novel. Because a few moments alone with you leaves me unable to think of anything to say save romantic nonsense that would make you laugh.* Wait! Charles had said that making women laugh was a good thing.

Prudence hoped he would not think much longer and wondered what it was he was thinking about. Oh, dear. He was almost too handsome to view at such close range with no one else present in the room as a distraction. She found she could not look away.

"Because you would do it well, Miss Reese," he said at last.

"If only that were true."

"What exactly is the problem? Would it help you to talk about it? I am not a writer, of course, but I can be an excellent listener."

She suppressed a snort and studied him for a long moment. "We have never really talked, you know."

"We could try, Miss Reese. I understand it is not difficult." His other relationships with women had not involved a great deal of talking, that was the trouble.

"I suppose you are right," she said carefully. "What shall we talk about?"

He thought again of Charles's advice, realizing with delight that he actually did have something to apologize for. "First, I would like to say how sorry I am."

She gave him a startled look. "What?"

"I suspect you think I do not take you seriously. Several weeks ago I dismissed the idea of your writing a novel in no uncertain terms and I have regretted it ever since. Many women write novels. There seems to be no stopping them. Why should you not do the same?"

Nettled, she tipped up her chin. "Your apology is far from flattering, Lord Alwyn. Indeed, it may be worse than the original offense."

He turned a faint shade of pink that matched the chair he was sitting in. "Must I apologize for my apology?" Charles had not mentioned this possible complication. "I have not your way with words, Miss Reese."

She softened her tone. "No, let it be. I own that I must apologize to you."

"Why? Surely *you* have done nothing, Miss Reese."

"I accused you of something you did not do."

He could not think what that might be; then understanding dawned in his befuddled brain. "Oho! You must mean the mysterious appearance of those drawings in the bishop's book. No, I did not hide them there."

"I found another copy of *Moral Discourses* in Mr. Furnivall's shop, upon the wrong shelf. The next five pictures in the series were tucked inside. I realized at that moment that it would have been impossible for you to have placed them there for me to find."

"Hallelujah," he said. "So I shall not be hanged at Tyburn after all."

"No—not that there was ever any danger of that, Lord Alwyn."

He thought it over. "I suspect that a printer's boy played a prank."

Prudence merely nodded, inwardly astonished at how readily he had guessed the answer, but unwilling to confide her conversation with Miss Sparks.

"It was sheer coincidence that you happened to find both sets, Miss Reese."

She nodded. "Yes. An amazing coincidence."

"Just so," he said smugly. "I am glad to be exonerated. And I should like to see the new ones."

The thought of looking at those sensual drawings with him made her tremble. She stiffened her back and answered him primly. "They are under lock and key in my room."

"Dear me," said Lord Alwyn. "Thank you for protecting my virtue, Miss Reese. Bishop Applegate would certainly approve. Reverend Ponsonby would applaud."

"You would not tell them of the drawings, would you?"

"Of course not. Though I suppose it would make no difference. They would hold me responsible and not you, since they regard me as a sinner beyond saving."

He leaned ever so slightly closer to her and Prudence did not move away. She knew nothing of sin, but if this irresistible man was indeed a sinner, she would like to know more.

She turned her face up to his, hoping that—

Lady Agatha came back into the room. That was *not* what Prudence had been hoping for. Alwyn sat back and frowned.

She was followed by Mrs. Dawkins, who carried an armful of newspapers and dragged a mop, to the great amusement of the five kittens in her wake.

They pounced upon its trailing strings and got tangled up, then jumped on for a ride.

"Quite a parade," Lord Alwyn said dryly. "Surely a small spill does not require this much fuss."

"Mrs. Dawkins wanted to be sure it was done right. She knows how fond I am of this carpet." Lady Agatha traced part of its garish design with the toe of one slipper. "And parting with the kittens is not easy for her—do be more kind, Alwyn."

"Milady, yer son is always very kind. Do not scold 'im on my account." The cook set down the newspapers and looked about for the supposed stain while the kittens scampered off.

"Very well, Mrs. Dawkins." Lady Agatha settled herself in the foliage throne once more and engaged Prudence in small talk about the weather.

Lord Alwyn watched Mrs. Dawkins come closer, mop at the ready. He lifted his boots and held his legs straight out, so as not to be in her way, annoyed that Prudence stifled a giggle at the sight.

There seemed to be absolutely no way to preserve his dignity in her presence. Every time they met, it turned into a scene from a comic operetta. *Swump-swump. Swump-swump.* The cook mopped under and around his chair. "There, sir. No 'arm done."

She left, forgetting the newspapers. Lady Agatha glanced idly at the one on top when she set down her teacup. "Oh! The latest *Bee*—what a treat! My dear Prudence, do you read Mrs. Motherwit's column?"

It was Miss Reese's turn to look embarrassed but why she was, Lord Alwyn did not know. Her cheeks had turned scarlet. "On occasion. Do you enjoy her, Lady Agatha?"

"I do indeed. And the Scourge of Whitehall as

well. I know that is Mr. Furnivall's nom de plume, but I have no idea who Mrs. Motherwit might be."

"What does it matter? So long as you enjoy it— that is the important thing," Prudence said quickly.

"Of course, dear," said Lady Agatha. "Oh!" She laughed out loud. "Mrs. Motherwit is most amusing today. Here is a husband caught in—"

"*Flagrante delicto*. I have read it," said Alwyn, a little stiffly.

His mother peered at him for a long moment. "And I thought you only read architectural treatises, Alwyn. Are you quite well?"

"Yes. Now that the library is nearly done, I have more time for leisurely pursuits."

"That is all to the good. I was thinking that perhaps you might take Miss Reese upon a tour of the building. I do not believe she has walked out for some time, or at least, not in that direction."

"I should be happy to, Mama. Miss Reese, are you agreeable to that plan?"

Prudence murmured her assent. She had spent far too much time indoors of late—or at the bookshop—and she would turn quickly into an old lady if she did not see the light of day once in a while and have a little fun.

She rose to remove a kitten that had climbed the draperies at the window. As soon as she set it upon the floor, another took its place, climbing higher still. Lord Alwyn seized the opportunity to admire Prudence's graceful figure, since his mother was reading.

Lady Agatha rattled the newspaper and seemed not to see either one of them. She studied the column again. "Hm. This is a silly one. Is this fellow madly in love with gingerbread—or with the young lady who makes it? Still, Mrs. Motherwit's answer is to the point."

"I read that one as well, Mama. And I'm sure that Miss Reese has too."

Prudence merely nodded. What if they knew that she had written it? She could not even bring herself to imagine the ensuing fuss.

"Am I boring you, Alwyn?" his mother asked.

"No. Not at all."

"You are tactful, dear boy. Now ring for Cathy and off you go. She can carry Herrick's kitten—Mrs. Dawkins says he is to have the orange one—and anything else you or Miss Reese might need."

The old lady looked at the mountain of cakes, which their hasty tea had scarcely diminished. "And do take some of these with you as well. No doubt the workmen will enjoy them."

Lord Alwyn looked at her with astonishment. "You have changed your tune about them, Mama."

The old lady merely shrugged. "I have my reasons, Alwyn."

She rang for Broderick, who gathered up the tea things on the tray along with the orange kitten.

They exchanged adieux, and Lady Agatha was alone at last. She waited several minutes, then went to the window to see the three of them walk down the street. Lord Alwyn and Miss Reese walked arm-in-arm—it was about time!—and Cathy was just behind, struggling to keep a curious kitten in a small basket while she hung onto a much larger one that undoubtedly held the cakes.

Lady Agatha had never been patient—and she was certainly not patient enough to wait and see what would happen between her son and Miss Reese if left to their own devices.

For all that Alwyn deserved his reputation as a rake, he seemed never to have been in love before now, and truly, he was as awkward as a schoolboy about it. He seemed not to have the least idea that men and women might simply enjoy themselves innocently enough and that such enjoyment could lead to lasting love.

Devoted to him as Lady Agatha was, she was doing her best, of course, and had been from the very first. For example, she had not scolded him for being in Miss Reese's room in his drawers. Things seemed to have slowed down dreadfully even after that auspicious beginning, however. Still, she reminded herself, both Alwyn and Prudence had been preoccupied by other matters.

But all that was unimportant in her grand scheme, though she could not do much more than provide opportunities. She had left them alone in the jungle room long enough to steal a kiss.

The room had been kept closed up long enough, after Reverend Ponsonby pointed out that its wild décor might stimulate animal instincts. Perhaps today it had—well and good.

The next step in her nefarious plan to make them have fun was the stroll through his library. The great booby might never have asked Prudence to accompany him thither if she had not interfered. Prudence was bound to be impressed, if Alwyn did not talk her ears off about architectural theory. And he did seem to be making an effort to be pleasant, even amusing. That would certainly help.

That he was wildly attracted to Prudence and vice versa, Lady Agatha had no doubt. He needed a well-placed kick in his buckskins, perhaps, to speed things along, and since his father was dead, that responsibility fell to her.

He could consider himself kicked. There was nothing wrong with that, in her opinion. Not even the Right Reverend Ponsonby would object. He was always going on about being fruitful and multiplying and so forth.

She watched them walk around the corner and out of sight, then settled down again to plan a menu for dinner in that worthy cleric's honor.

Chapter Thirteen

"Hoi! It is Lord Alwyn!" The men upon the roof waved in greeting.

Prudence was astonished to see that the façade was in place and that a row of attached columns, topped with a pediment in restrained classical style, now framed an ornate double door. Carpenters were installing high windows that would flood the rooms with light.

Behind the façade she could see the reading room dome, clad with copper sheets that blazed in the sun.

"Would you like a closer look?" Alwyn asked proudly. "The door has been decorated with allegories of learning, scenes from Aesop's fables and so forth. It is a remarkable piece of carving."

"Yes, if I may," said Prudence. "Come, Cathy." She turned to see the maid clap the lid on the little basket and drop the large one. The kitten was once more attempting to escape. "Oh, dear. Let me help you."

"Herrick!" Lord Alwyn bellowed. Prudence winced. She had almost forgotten how loudly he could yell. "We come bearing gifts!"

The breeze took Cathy's bonnet and down tumbled her red hair just as the master builder appeared. Herrick took one look at her, and his rugged face became tender. "Thank ye, sir. Good day, Miss Reese—and Miss Cathy."

"Do you know each other? Well, no matter—here is the kitten and here are cakes!" Alwyn took both baskets from Cathy and handed them over.

"In a manner of speaking, yes, we do, sir. Her brother works for me." The lid of the basket rose a few inches and the kitten scrambled up the master builder's leather vest and quickly reached his brawny shoulder.

"A bold fellow!" Herrick said with an approving smile.

The sight of the roughly dressed builder and his kitten drew rude shouts from the men upon the roof.

"Get back to work! Have ye never seen a kitten afore?" As they were well out of reach of the swing of his fists they continued to tease him mercilessly.

"Are ye daft, Herrick?"

"Eatin' stray cats fer lunch?"

"Who is the lydy wif the red hair?"

"Does she fancy you?" The last comment caused a burst of raucous laughter but the master builder ignored it. "Tell her brother, someone!"

Prudence looked closely at the blushing maid. "Oh! This must be the brother who makes candy and mixes mortar!"

"Not at the same time, I hope," Lord Alwyn joked.

"Nay," Herrick said. He could not take his eyes from Cathy's face, even though the kitten had decided to stroll, by way of his unprotected neck, to his other shoulder to see if the view was better from there.

"You did not tell me your brother worked here," Prudence said. "What is his name?"

"William," Herrick said. "She brings 'im lunch each day and a very good lunch it is. Hespecially the gingerbread."

"Thank you, Mr. Herrick," Cathy said shyly. "William told me you liked it. As it happens, we have brought some."

"Ah. I am a lucky man." Herrick's next words came out rather in a rush. "Ye are as pretty as a picture, like a lady at Vauxhall—have ye ever been there?—and ye can cook. Would ye mind, sir, if I spoke to Miss Cathy alone?" He looked meaningfully at Lord Alwyn.

"Not at all," Alwyn replied. He turned to walk away and took Prudence with him by the simple method of taking her soft arm into his hand. "Shall we look at the door?"

They were barely ten steps away when he took the added liberty of whispering in her ear, which tickled very pleasantly since Disappearing Joseph had not done a particularly good job of shaving him this morning.

"Miss Reese, this is amazing!"

"It is indeed a remarkable door," she whispered back, "but why did you pull me away?"

"Do you not realize—oh, this is most entertaining! And Mrs. Dawkins was right!"

"Whatever are you talking about?"

"She insisted that Mrs. Motherwit was a real person—and now we know that *Herrick* is the Invisible Man who wrote that letter! You read it, did you not? It all fits: the gingerbread, the shy beauty, the longing looks, Vauxhall, et cetera."

Prudence's lips parted with astonishment. She

knew only too well, of course, that Mrs. Motherwit was a real person, but it had somehow not occurred to her that she might actually meet some of her correspondents. Looking at the happy faces of Herrick and Cathy gave her a sinking feeling. They did not know that *she* had advised the master builder to woo and win his fair lady. She hoped they never would.

It was all too close for comfort. And so was Lord Alwyn.

"Come with me," he said. "You have never been here, have you?"

"No, I have not."

They entered the front hall and she mentally compared the plans she had seen with the actual building. It was the same, certainly, in its outlines but no two-dimensional drawing could capture the effect of grandeur his design evoked.

Though the library took up but two building lots, the interior columns and the reading room dome they supported made it seem far more spacious. A team of carpenters moved about the inside scaffolding, putting up strong shelves that nearly reached the ceiling and bookcases that seemed longer than a milc.

"How will anyone reach the books on the top?" she asked.

"We will build connecting galleries, my dear, and stairs to them."

Had he really called her *my dear*? Prudence decided she must not have heard him correctly. He seemed aglow with pride and his speech was rapid.

"I see. You must not let children play upon those. They will run round and round the gallery, just for fun. But perhaps you might add a room just for them—"

"A capital idea!" he interrupted. "And entirely new, as far as I know. The Purcell Library shall have the first room for children in London. What made you think of it, Miss Reese?"

"You once mentioned reading to your young cousins—fairy tales, was it?"

He nodded. "Yes. I still have those tattered old volumes but we will need hundreds of new ones. Children are hard on books, what with their sticky little hands and penchant for cutting out interesting pictures."

Prudence, who had done quite a lot of that in her childhood, agreed with a nod.

"Would you like to pick the books?"

"I should like that very much," Prudence said. "Mr. Furnivall will be glad of our custom. And his assistant seems to know the title of every book ever published. She has tremendous powers of recall and she has been a great help to me—" Prudence stopped herself from explaining in what way.

Miss Sparks's extraordinary memory had provided Prudence with all books she needed to help her sound as wise as Mrs. Motherwit was supposed to be. Since so many people read the column, she wanted to be sure that the advice she offered was sound, even if the questions were not.

Lord Alwyn and Prudence had passed through the first rooms and were now entering the back of the building, where rare and valuable volumes would be stored for the use of scholars and clergymen. Here the walls were thicker and there were fewer windows; the room was designed to protect books that could not easily be replaced.

Small niches had been built into the walls, so that books might be studied without being removed.

They went by several, turned a corner, and nearly ran into Herrick and Cathy.

"Beggin' yer pardon, sir," said Herrick nervously.

"No need," said Lord Alwyn.

"Ye must've wondered where I was," Herrick said.

"No, I did not," Lord Alwyn said. "Miss Reese and I were quite content to be alone."

The other man nodded. "I take yer meaning, sir. But me and Cathy was thinking of going upon the roof. The men are about to break for the day—they are feeding that kitten the remains of their lunches and I don't know where the hungry little bugger puts it, beggin' your pardon, Miss Reese—but I thought we might take the air."

Lord Alwyn nodded. "Why not? If these two ladies can climb a scaffold, we can see the sunset from there. If they cannot, then we shall throw them over our shoulders to carry them up and save them the trouble."

"Oh! Indeed not!" Prudence said. "We shall go up on our own. I am not afraid of heights. Are you, Cathy?"

The maid shook her head.

"Very good." Alwyn led Prudence to a contrived affair of planks and poles and rickety ladders. "Are you sure, my dear?"

There was no mistaking that *my dear.* He had said it. And there was no mistaking the gleam in his eye. The breeze had not died down, Prudence noticed. No doubt Lord Alwyn fully expected to catch a glimpse of her pantaloons.

She paused and asked herself what Mrs. Motherwit would say to a girl in her situation. Surely the good old lady would advise against it on the grounds of propriety and common sense. Yet spending time—any amount of time—with Lord Alwyn seemed to dissolve both.

Prudence put one foot upon the first rung of the rickety ladder and pulled herself up to the next.

She reached the roof a little dustier than when she began but triumphant, and was shortly joined by Cathy, whose red hair gleamed in the fading light of day. They had proceeded up the scaffolding at a pace that made peeking at anyone's pantaloons impossible, as the men had been forced to follow them just as quickly.

The four were in high spirits by the time all had reached the roof.

"Oh my!" said Cathy in wonderment, "I have never been up so high! Look, there is the Thames! And St. Paul's, there in the distance! Oh my!"

She turned about, making herself giddy, until Herrick caught her arm.

"Steady, miss. It takes some getting used to."

He pointed out other landmarks as Prudence walked around the immense, copper-clad dome to the side that faced Lady Agatha's house. So this was what Alwyn had seen from the basket when the walls were first rising. She looked into the top floor window, just able to make out the sofa where his mother had fallen asleep on that long-ago day.

Her hair had come down in the mad dash to the roof and it now blew about her face. Lord Alwyn approached and reached up a hand to smooth it back. His gentleness surprised her. He said nothing for a moment, looking at her and then away. Then he spoke.

"We will have to go down at once. The sun is setting

and it is not safe in the dark." He took her hand. They walked around the dome together and back to the others.

"There ye be, sir. I was worried for a moment."

"We must hurry down. Herrick, lead the way."

Cathy protested briefly, but when the sun rested upon the horizon and began to slip away she said no more. Herrick climbed down and waited for her to follow. They soon disappeared below the roofline.

"I hate to leave." Prudence turned for one last, long look at London. "May I return someday?" she asked softly. "I like it up here. It seems we have spent many happy hours upon rooftops."

"That is true, Miss Reese. And I hope to spend many more." He hoped to have a lifetime of such happiness with her. And why not start with a kiss? She turned her lovely face to him, and he captured it between his hands.

"Oh!" Her lips parted.

"My dear Prudence! If I may—"

She knew what was coming and gave herself up, body and soul, to him.

In but a moment Prudence found herself being expertly and tenderly kissed. There was no hesitation on his part this time, no holding back on hers. Lord Alwyn seemed to have only one thought, and that was of her pleasure.

Refusing him, pushing him away, playing coy games was the last thing on her mind. Though an innocent in such matters, she knew that she wanted him with all her heart.

He held her close for what seemed to be hours afterward, but of course it was only minutes. The sheer wonder and perilous joy of being desired so ardently had addled her wits. Very good. She hoped he would continue to addle them. She loved the sensation of being swept off her feet. She had just been compromised in the most *delicious* way.

"My darling," he whispered. "Now I must marry you. And you must say yes. Doesn't that work out nicely?"

"Indeed it does, my lord," she whispered back. "But you haven't asked properly."

He set her aside and dropped to one knee, keeping her hand in his. "My dear Prudence," he began. "With the moon and the stars as witness—"

"They haven't come out yet." She looked up at the deep blue heaven above. "No—wait. There is one."

This twinkling jewel was low in the sky and all alone.

"That is Venus," Lord Alwyn said. "How fitting. I pledge my heart to you with the goddess of love as witness. We shall be married in a few weeks' time, my dearest Prudence." He rose, and kissed her again with all the passion he possessed.

Prudence was swept off her feet a second time. And a third. Then they heard Herrick calling anxiously for them and broke apart, running hand in hand to the scaffolding to join the others.

Chapter Fourteen

Prudence awoke with a headache. There was something she was supposed to do today, but she could not remember it. Alwyn's kiss—oh, what a kiss that was!—and their dizzying descent in the dark had quite wrecked her ability to think.

She had made the mistake of looking down and seen nothing but blackness. Too frightened to continue, she had let him carry her with one strong arm about her waist. How they reached the ground in one piece, she did not know. *Part luck, part love*, she thought dreamily.

She had nearly swooned in his embrace, but recovered somewhat when her feet touched the ground. Cathy had pressed a wet cloth to her head and made her sit down. Then the men walked them home, and Mrs. Dawkins let them in the side door without saying one word about it.

"Proooo-dence!"

She sat bolt upright. Was she supposed to breakfast with Lady Agatha? The sun pouring through the windows told her that it was far too late for that.

The old lady knocked at the door and came in. "I did not see you when you came in last night, my dear. But then I was sleeping. The Reverend Ponsonby was telling me of his latest scheme and I simply lost interest and drifted off. Broderick showed him out. I do hope he is not too offended."

"Are you not planning a dinner in his honor, Lady Agatha?" There, she remembered that much, Prudence thought.

"Yes. I have decided upon the menu—and I shall order the best madeira from Dibbles & Hopping to make up for my falling asleep. Ponsonby does enjoy a drop of madeira, he says—but 'jest a drap.'" She imitated the clergyman's reedy voice and odd accent for comic effect, and Prudence smiled.

"You have roses in your cheeks, my dear." Lady Agatha said fondly. "I assume you slept well? Did you and Alwyn enjoy yourselves?"

Prudence answered *that* question as calmly as she could. "Oh—yes. The library is most impressive. I had no idea. The houses near yours block much of our view of it. Lord Alwyn took me through the front hall and the reading room and the vaults—it is a great work indeed."

Strangely, she did not feel in the least bit jealous that he would certainly finish his project first. In fact, all her feelings for Lord Alwyn were of the most delicious, positively passionate kind. She stretched a bit, feeling rather like singing.

"I am glad you are rested, Prudence. Mr. Furnivall sent round more boxes of books—oh, do not scowl so! Cathy will help me with those. But he sent a note to remind you to meet him and Miss Sparks at the shop. What is that about, my dear?"

To save her life, Prudence could not remember. She thought hard. Something to do with Mrs. Motherwit, of course . . . but exactly what escaped her.

"Never mind. I will ask Cathy to bring up your tea

and breakfast in bed. Nothing is finer than breakfast in bed, and you may wake up at your leisure."

"Thank you, Lady Agatha. I will be down presently." Prudence slipped back under the covers as the old lady left.

Nothing was finer—except breakfast in bed with Lord Alwyn, and they would soon be sharing that. His whispered promise—and proposal—last night had gladdened her heart, and his caresses had thrilled her to her very fingertips. But of course she would not breathe a word of their secret engagement to his dear mama. Not yet.

Accompanied by Cathy, Prudence walked to Chiswell Street and was surprised to see a crowd gathered outside the shop window. What was going on? Why the commotion? Onlookers jostled each other and more people stopped to see.

As they approached the edge of the crowd, Prudence suddenly remembered Mr. Furnivall's plans to print a collection of earlier columns by Mrs. Motherwit. She was relieved that she had not been writing long enough to be included. The bookseller hoped to capitalize upon the ever-growing popularity of his fictional beldam. But surely a mere pile of books in a shop window would not excite so much attention.

She stood on her tiptoes to see over a burly man and her mouth opened in an O. There was Miss Sparks, sitting upon an overstuffed chair in the window by a small desk, dipping a quill into a bottle of ink and signing whatever was thrust under her nose.

She was decked out in mobcap and spectacles, striped dress and apron, and was doing a credible impersonation of the imaginary columnist. A happy mob of customers was waiting to talk to her. Some held old copies of the *Bee* for her to autograph.

Prudence and Cathy would have to get inside to hear what she was saying, which would take a little time. Cathy went first, squeezing her way through the crowd and pushing the rougher men aside so that her mistress might pass.

A little breathless, they gained the dim interior of the shop and looked for Mr. Furnivall. He was nowhere to be seen. But they could hear Miss Sparks answering questions. Prudence squeezed through the crowd once more and made her way toward her, leaving Cathy behind to fend off Eggy Weems, who seemed not to have lost his bad habit of popping up where he wasn't wanted.

"Mrs. Motherwit! D'ye remember me? I was Bad Behavior in Barkingdale!" called out a middle-aged man in an ill-fitting suit of corduroy.

"Bad Behavior in Barkingdale. February 17, 1812," said Miss Sparks. "I told you to turn over a new leaf, did I not?"

"Yes! And d'ye know, my sweetheart married me, just like ye said!"

"Congratulations."

"We have seven children, Mrs. Motherwit."

Miss Sparks cast him a horrified look and adjusted her spectacles. "You have my sympathy, sir."

"Mrs. Motherwit! Mrs. Motherwit! I am next! I was Vexed in Essex!"

"Vexed in Essex. May 9, 1812. You had difficulties with your mother-in-law. I told you to be patient."

"That's right, Mrs. Motherwit! You are a wonder! It worked!"

"What exactly did you do?" Miss Sparks inquired.

"We had nine children—two sets of twins—in seven years. Me mother-in-law left soon enough," said the other woman. Prudence noted her trim waist. It scarcely seemed possible that she'd produced so many, but Prudence's brief stint as Mrs. Motherwit had taught her that anything was possible.

"Goodness," said Miss Sparks. "I believe your mother-in-law wrote to me as well. She was . . . Inundated With Infants, November 13, 1814."

"Mrs. Motherwit! Mrs. Motherwit!" In the general clamor, neither Prudence nor Cathy, still some distance away, noted the appearance of Mr. Furnivall. He made his way to Prudence's side.

"Miss Sparks truly is a wonder. She remembers every column from the first to the last," he said softly.

"Oh!" said Prudence. "You gave me a start, Mr. Furnivall. Yes, she is—and she has attracted quite a crowd. I seem to remember you telling me about the printed collection of Motherwit columns, but not this."

"The idea came to me suddenly—and when Miss Sparks agreed, I sent her out for the costume. I was hoping you could help her, but I think she has done admirably on her own."

Prudence nodded. "She seems to be in her element."

"The sales of the book will drive up sales of the *Bee*, Miss Reese. And your columns are even more popular than the previous Mrs. Motherwit's. Perhaps we will issue a collection of yours next."

"Thank you—but I am not at all sure I want to continue."

The bookseller's face fell. "Oh, dear. How much longer do I have?"

Prudence felt a flash of remorse but she could not very well be the wife of a sought-after architect and keep up with such a flood of correspondence.

And she would be Alwyn's wife within a matter of weeks. He had promised her that, in the tenderest of whispers.

Prudence would never tell him that she had scribbled a few columns for the *Bee.* Although there was no shame in such work, it would be thought odd in the circles in which he hoped to move.

She had become Mrs. Motherwit on a mad impulse, just to earn a bit of money. And she did not regret it—she had learned much. Now, perhaps, she could write a novel. That was something that could be done at any time, as she pleased, and not under the pressure of a newspaper deadline.

She imagined herself at her blue desk once more—in a new house, which Alwyn would build just for her—but her fantasy was interrupted by Mr. Furnivall's soft voice.

"How much time do I have?" he repeated.

"Oh dear, I was daydreaming. It is very warm in here, Mr. Furnivall. If I might sit down?" She looked over to Cathy, who kept Eggy at bay apparently by treading on his feet. Prudence saw him step back and heard his faint "Ow!"

"Certainly." For an old man, Mr. Furnivall showed surprising strength as he elbowed his way and hers through the crowd. They arrived at his office in the rear and she waved to Cathy to wait.

Prudence perched on a small chair that seemed to have been upholstered with ink stains. Truly, she would not miss the grubbiness of publishing and writing books. She had no idea why anyone thought of it as glamorous.

"I will continue to write until you hire a replacement, Mr. Furnivall. But you must find someone soon."

"Have you not enjoyed the work, Miss Reese?" he said smoothly. "I am not sure I could easily find another writer of your caliber."

She steeled herself against his flattery, knowing from experience what an old sneak he was.

"My reasons for leaving are personal, Mr. Furnivall." She gave him a demure smile.

"I see. Then I shall not pry, Miss Reese. I suppose we must return to the fray."

The noise inside the shop was growing louder.

"Yes, and I must rescue Cathy."

She rose and they left the office together. Prudence made her way to Cathy's side and scowled at Eggy. She noted belatedly that he held the hand of a smaller boy she had not seen in the crowd.

"Cathy, this is Eggy."

"Pleased to make yer acquaintance, miss, even if ye did step on me feet twice. This here is me brother. His name is—"

"Not Bacon, I hope," Cathy said crossly.

Eggy made a yurking noise that Prudence supposed was his way of laughing. "Naow. His name is just plain Bob."

Bob looked nothing at all like Eggy, fortunately for him. He favored both young women with a gap-toothed grin. It was endearing in an odd way—Prudence hoped that he would not grow up to be as obnoxious as his brother.

"By the bye, Miss Reese . . . ye once said something to me about discretion. I could continue to assure ye of it, should ye happen to find a shilling or two before ye leave. Or three." He smiled and waited for his bribe.

She stiffened. "Pray excuse me for a moment, Cathy. I will explain later."

The maid cast an angry look at Eggy and backed away, keeping an eye on her mistress. Prudence gestured for her to turn around, and Cathy obeyed, though reluctantly. Prudence rummaged in her reticule.

There was a tuppence at the bottom, and nothing more. She gave it to Eggy anyway. He handed it to his brother as if the coin were beneath his status as an amateur blackmailer, and returned his expectant gaze to Prudence.

"Oh!" she said, angry with herself and with him. She was half-tempted to publicly accuse him of putting the amorous drawings in the bishop's book but what earthly good would that do? "Go to the devil! I don't care who you tell!"

Prudence and Cathy began to make their way to the door once more, and burst out into the street with a sigh of relief. Prudence paused to get her breath—and was confronted by a familiar waistcoat. She had nestled against it only last night.

She looked up.

Lord Alwyn looked down.

They spoke simultaneously. "What are you doing here?"

Chapter Fifteen

Lord Alwyn hesitated. He had been to another print dealer not far from Chiswell Street, who had promised him the remaining five drawings of the couple in the garden. How this dealer had come by them, he would not say—but he was charging a pretty penny, since he had correctly guessed that Lord Alwyn would pay dearly.

He planned to have them bound in morocco leather and to tuck the book under Prudence's pillow on their wedding night. All in all, not an explanation he wanted to make in public.

But what was Prudence doing here? He was glad to see that Cathy was with her.

He looked into the shop window and saw Miss Sparks. Her spectacles were askew and her gray bun was disintegrating into wisps. Yet she soldiered on, signing autographs and answering questions from a throng of people.

Alwyn noticed the sign upon the desk at her side. *Meet Mrs. Motherwit!* He smiled, bemused. "So she is real."

"In a manner of speaking, yes," Prudence said nervously.

"I must tell Mrs. Dawkins. She will be here in a twinkling."

"Oh no—do not tell Mrs. Dawkins—please, Alwyn!"

He looked at her, mystified. "As you wish, my dear. But I might obtain an autograph on her behalf—she would like that."

Cathy was shoved in the rudest way. She whirled around, ready to whack the culprit—and stopped. It was Eggy Weems, still dragging his little brother by the hand.

"Beggin' yer pardon, guv'nor," Eggy said. "There is more than one Mrs. Motherwit."

Alwyn was shocked to see how this news upset Prudence. "My dear Pru—Miss Reese—surely you do not know this young lout?"

"'Course she does, guv'nor. And I know 'er. She is the other one." Eggy smiled wickedly. "The other Mrs. Motherwit—the real one."

Alwyn stared at Miss Sparks and then at Prudence, who was flushed and trembling. "You?"

"For only a little while, Alwyn!" She bit her lip, holding back tears.

"So that explains the Furnivall connection—and the mysterious letters."

"What?"

"I saw you writing them once. Do you know, this revelation is a welcome one! Silly girl . . . you are as impulsive as Mama but I love you anyway. You can explain it all later. Not here, dearest." Alwyn folded her into his arms, where she began to cry in earnest, wetting his waistcoat. He did not care.

Eggy whistled nonchalantly. "Who's sorry now? Where's me shilling, eh?"

Prudence gave a miserable howl and Eggy laughed. Alwyn let go of Prudence, detached the younger boy from Eggy's hand, lifted the gangly lad up by his collar, and threw him in the gutter without a moment's hesitation. Bob crept behind Cathy's skirts and stayed there.

"Ow! Ow! He kilt me! Or tried to!" Eggy rolled about in the muck.

"Be off!" thundered Alwyn. The mob of people turned from the shop window and stared at Eggy, who scrambled to his feet and ran for it. They turned back when he had disappeared, quickly losing interest in the scuffle.

The little boy who had hidden himself behind Cathy peeped out. He was crying too. "Eggy is not me brother, miss. He said to say that or he would hit me. He named me Bob. He were going to teach me to pick pockets but I didn't want to."

Alwyn let go of Prudence, handing her his handkerchief, and bent to talk to the boy. "Where are your parents, lad?"

"Dead, sir. And me gran, too. Last week. I had no food and no place to stay."

"Come with us," Cathy said suddenly. "You do now. And you are going to like Mrs. Dawkins."

Alwyn looked at her and at Prudence, momentarily bewildered. "How do you know the boy is telling the truth?"

"He is too young to lie about such things, sir," she said simply. "He is no more than six, I am sure of it."

"What is your name?" he asked the boy.

"Percival," the little fellow said proudly.

"And your last name?"

"I do not know it, sir."

"He is frank enough. Perhaps you are right, Cathy. Prudence, what do you think?"

"We cannot just ignore a problem and hope it will go away. Mrs. Motherwit would not." She took one of the little boy's hands and Cathy took the other. "He is too small to walk all the way home with us."

Lord Alwyn went to fetch a cab.

Chapter Sixteen

Several days later . . .

Young Percival had quickly learned his way about the Purcell household, thought Lord Alwyn, adapting to its eccentric routines with ease.

He was a likely lad, despite his sad beginnings—his story had been confirmed by a Bow Street runner sent to the East End streets where the boy had grown up.

Percival had been fortunate, indeed, to meet the soft-hearted Cathy in his moment of need. The streets of London were full of such children, with no one to look after them, forced into a life of miserable servitude, petty crime, and worse.

But Percival was safe and happy here. The boy especially liked the jungle room and took particular care dusting the furniture in it when charged with that task by Mrs. Dawkins. Perhaps he liked it because he was a bit of a monkey, always sliding down the banisters and scrambling up the trellises just as Alwyn had done at the same age.

The other page, the one who was always sleeping, had seized the occasion of Percival's arrival to run away and join the circus along with Disappearing Joseph.

It was no great loss, as far as the valet went. Alwyn did a rather better job of shaving by himself. He hoped the boy would enjoy the circus, though he suspected he would be set to mucking out the elephants' stalls before he got to ride any.

Lady Agatha had asked after the missing page only once, and even then she had not remembered his name—only recalling that he took more naps than she did.

But Percival was doted upon by Mrs. Dawkins and had become Cathy's pet. He often followed her, pleading to help and working hard when she allowed him to.

Cathy went about her work with a song on her lips now that she was Herrick's one and only. Being in love did amazing things for women.

Prudence, too, was blooming. The ridiculous business of the advice column had been tearfully explained and manfully forgiven. Alwyn had made the most of it, holding her close as long as he dared, though his mother was no longer quite so quick to interrupt them in the name of propriety.

Lady Agatha had not been told of their secret engagement in so many words, but she seemed to have guessed. There were times, Alwyn owned, when his scatterbrained mother seemed to know exactly what to do.

And there were times when she didn't. If only he could make her understand that Reverend Ponsonby was not to be trusted. But she remained stubbornly attached to the man. The thought of Ponsonby's absurd motto, engraved upon the cornerstone where everyone could see it, made Alwyn impossibly cross. After all, he thought, it was his library, not Ponsonby's—even if his mother called it hers.

Perhaps it would be the better part of wisdom to call it *the* library and be done with it.

The library was done, in any case. Alwyn had thought finishing it would be the high point of his life, but the day had come and gone like any other despite the workmen's noisy celebration.

No, the high point of his life had happened well before the library's completion when he kissed— really kissed—the passionate Miss Prudence. He could not wait to marry her.

The table had been set for the great dinner—the meeting of minds—the ecumenical repast—or whatever Lady Agatha was calling it now. The high and mighty Bishop Applegate would walk through the doors of Purcell House in less than an hour, turn sharply left into the best dining room and take his place above the salt.

The Right Reverend Ponsonby would be seated across the table. Prudence would be next to him and facing Alwyn, she knew. He refused point-blank to sit next to Ponsonby. Lady Agatha would preside with all due ceremony. She hoped she could stay awake.

That brave hope receded as the evening wore on. Prudence forced her eyes open at the sound of Applegate's sonorous voice.

"Is this fish or fowl, my dear lady?" The bishop squinted at the platter that had just been presented by Broderick, furrowing his forehead. "I fear that a rich sauce has been too liberally applied. There is no telling what lies underneath."

Reverend Ponsonby frowned at it as well. "Exactly. Like the young women of today, so fair and yet so often false. A virtuous man is in constant danger from all sorts of wickedness. If we can interpret the lesson in the fish upon this platter, we see that God wants us to—"

"I beg your pardon?" Lady Agatha looked anxiously between the two clergymen. "Surely a fillet of flounder is not so menacing as all that."

"Of course not, dear Lady Agatha," the bishop said. "My distinguished colleague is drawing an analogy. His reasoning may be too subtle for a female mind."

"Reverend Ponsonby seems to find the subject of female wickedness quite fascinating," Alwyn said. "He talks of little else." He rolled his eyes for Prudence's benefit. She, rosy-cheeked from two glasses of excellent madeira to Alwyn's five, held back a giggle.

Emboldened by her appreciation, he went on. "And how is it, Ponsonby, that you know so much about what God wants of us?"

The reverend ignored this jab and addressed his next remarks to his hostess. "My dear Lady Agatha," Ponsonby said gravely. "We may see signs of the Almighty's wisdom everywhere, if we only but look." He picked up an apple from the centerpiece. "Here we have an ordinary apple. Yet this humble fruit is also a reminder of mankind's fall from grace."

Lord Alwyn took it from his hand and bit into it with a juicy crunch. "And very good it is, too."

Prudence laughed outright, then quickly clapped a hand over her mouth. She looked down the table to Lady Agatha. Wonder of wonders, the old lady was wrestling with a smile that would not go away.

"Broderick, bring in the next dish," she said

imperiously. "Make sure it is plain and dressed only with salt. No sauce. No parsley."

"Lady Agatha, have I offended you?" said the reverend. "I meant no criticism of your table. Your cook has prepared excellent food, for which I am abjectly grateful."

The man's fawning tone was giving Alwyn indigestion. He tried not to listen and winked at Prudence instead.

But Ponsonby attempted to engage him in conversation. "I understand that the library is finished, Lord Alwyn. I must say, I deplore the use of pagan elements in a structure that will bear my motto and name upon its cornerstone."

We shall see about that, Alwyn thought, but all he said was, "Are you referring to its classical design?"

"You may call the time of the ancient Greeks and Romans classical, but they *were* pagan," Ponsonby insisted.

"As they lived several centuries before the coming of Christ, they had little choice in the matter," said Alwyn tartly.

Prudence could see the reverend counting on his fingers under the table.

"Perhaps you have a point," Ponsonby conceded. "But I myself prefer the Gothic style for its echoes of holiness. My church is Gothic. My house is Gothic. My soul is Gothic."

"Your privy is Gothic, or so I understand," said Lord Alwyn.

"Alwyn!" said Lady Agatha, scandalized.

"It is true, Mama. It was written up in an architectural journal quite recently. Am I lying, Ponsonby?"

He bowed his head. "No, you are not. It seemed

to go with the house rather better than the ordinary kind."

Lady Agatha turned the conversation to a safer topic. "As you were saying, Bishop Applegate, the newspapers will print anything these days. I am loath to have them in the house. Except for the *Bee*."

"The morals of the reading public," the bishop began in a pompous tone somewhat compromised by a mouthful of fish, "are at grave risk. Murders and mayhem are everyday staples." He swallowed what was in his mouth and continued. "Abandoned women are openly admired, and tittle-tattle has replaced serious thought. Family secrets are revealed and dirty linen is aired for the amusement of all. I am thinking of Mrs. Motherwit's column, which I do not read, of course."

"Then how do you know what it says?" Prudence inquired, blaming the madeira for her impudence.

Reverend Ponsonby gave her hand a moist pat with his own. Alwyn saw her instantly withdraw it and hide it in her lap. No doubt she was wiping it upon her dress.

"There, there, my dear," Ponsonby said. "Do not trouble your pretty head about it. The bishop was speaking in a rhetorical sense. One does not have to read things to know what they say."

She merely shrugged and looked at Alwyn. The reverend seized the opportunity to cast a glance down her bodice.

Alwyn shot him an icy glare that seemed to surprise him. "Can't say that I follow that, Ponsonby. And do not pat Miss Reese, if you please."

The reverend seemed to grovel. No mean feat, thought Alwyn, as they were sitting at a well-appointed dinner table and there was no dirt to grovel in properly.

He might have to see to that. Alwyn continued to glare at Ponsonby, who added a cringe to the grovel.

"I meant no harm, sir. It was a gesture of brotherly affection."

"I must confess that I read Mrs. Motherwit from time to time," Lady Agatha changed the subject again. "I suppose most women do. Her frankness is refreshing and she is sometimes very amusing."

"Yet we must resist small temptations lest we give in to bigger ones," Bishop Applegate said. "Women are especially subject to this weakness."

"And men as well," said Ponsonby. "To be quite fair."

"Surely no woman could tempt a man whose heart is pure," Lord Alwyn pointed out. His sarcastic tone was quite lost on Ponsonby, he noticed.

The reverend sighed. "One has."

"Yes, well—you are a married man, of course," Lady Agatha said. "I assume that Mrs. Ponsonby was not unpleasing in her younger days."

The reverend shook his head. "It was not she."

At that moment, Cathy entered, bearing a curled-up piece of cooked beef, without sauce, upon a platter. Evidently she, who did not usually serve at dinner, had been quickly aproned and sent upstairs to accommodate Lady Agatha's last-minute request.

Cathy took one look at Ponsonby and dropped the platter. It shattered into a dozen pieces, and the piece of beef landed in the reverend's lap. "You!" She pointed an accusing finger at him.

The reverend turned pale.

"Whatever is the matter?" Lady Agatha inquired.

Prudence looked wide-eyed at Ponsonby and then at the bishop, who assumed a blameless expression—though he did seem interested in the drama unfolding before his eyes.

"Oh!" Cathy nearly screamed, then remembered where she was. "I—I was in service at the house of 'im and that poor Mrs. Ponsonby when I first came to London. He would not leave me alone until I hit 'im with the coal scuttle! 'Twas in the papers! I am Catherine Tipton!"

Prudence gasped. In all this time, she had never learned Cathy's last name—but she did remember that a Miss Tipton had done battle with the lecherous Reverend Ponsonby.

"Dear me," Lady Agatha said coldly, looking askance at Ponsonby, "is this true?"

He gingerly removed the piece of beef from his lap and draped it on the centerpiece, as there seemed to be no other place for it. "Yes. She tempted me. But I have forgiven her," he said sulkily.

"*You* forgave *her*? Ponsonby, I ought to thrash you!" Alwyn rose from his chair as if he were about to do just that, but Prudence shook her head to stop him.

"Was it not enough that I was pilloried in the penny press?" Ponsonby whined.

"No, you should have been run out of town. I would have been happy to lead the charge myself!" Alwyn said.

"My dear, do sit down," said Lady Agatha. "I think that Reverend Ponsonby can hang himself, given enough rope."

"What?" Ponsonby turned to his benefactress. "Seduction is not a hanging offense."

"I do not think it can be termed a seduction if your tender embraces were repulsed with a coal scuttle. It seems to me that you are trying to blame an innocent girl for what you did," Alwyn said. "Surely Cathy did not ask to be chased up and down the stairs—and worse."

"How do you know that, Alwyn?" Lady Agatha asked.

"I read the papers that you will not have in the house."

"I am glad to see that you keep up with current events," his mother said, somewhat acidly. "Why did you not tell me of this?"

Alwyn sighed. "I did not make the connection between the Miss Tipton in the newspaper accounts and Cathy. I knew only that you had hired her recently, upon the recommendation of Mrs. Dawkins, and that you were well pleased with her."

Lady Agatha cast a long and thoughtful look at the unrepentant sinner at her table. "Well, well. It is a good thing that the cornerstone has not been carved. Your name shall not be on it—or your idiotic motto. Your book of advice for young gentlewomen shall not be included in my library, Ponsonby. Our association is at an end!"

The bishop held up a hand. "Surely you can forgive him, Lady Agatha. The right reverend is fallible, like all men. Besides, can the word of a mere servant be trusted?"

Cathy interrupted him, wringing her hands. "I was not the first or the last maid he tried to take, mum. There were many others. You must believe me, Lady Agatha!"

The old lady fixed a thoughtful look upon the reverend, who squirmed in his chair.

He looked guilty, as well he might, for he had admitted his sin. But he had shown no remorse. Prudence understood Lady Agatha well enough to know how deeply this would anger her.

Lady Agatha threw down her serviette and rose from her chair. "I do believe you, Cathy. You have proved yourself to be a hardworking and honest girl." She gave Ponsonby a steely glare. "What are you waiting for? Out!"

For once in his life, the Right Reverend Ponsonby was at a loss for words. He got up, brushing bits of beef from his lap, and left through the door Broderick held open, followed by the bishop.

Then Ponsonby turned and looked sorrowfully at Lady Agatha. "We shall meet in heaven, dear lady." He wiped away a tear.

"Good gracious! I hope not!"

Alwyn nearly choked. Ponsonby regretted nothing more than losing Lady Agatha's patronage. And if it came to a battle between righteous indignation versus sniveling hypocrisy, Alwyn's money would be on his mother.

Broderick walked through the door, escorting Cathy out, and shut it from the other side. Prudence, Alwyn, and Lady Agatha sat back down, looked at each other—and began to laugh. And laugh. And laugh.

The reprehensible Ponsonby had received his comeuppance, and a servant girl had triumphed. It had been an interesting evening, after all.

"Oh, dear. Oh, goodness me." Lady Agatha's hilarity subsided. "From first to last, what a very odd dinner. Ponsonby is a fool and nothing more. His homily upon the flounder—his moralizing—his lugubrious expression—oh, dear!" She wiped her eyes. "And the bishop! What a pompous ass!"

"At last you understand why I dislike them both, Mama," Alwyn said. "Certainly I have nothing against the dear old Church of England, and the excellent men who serve in it. Their numbers are legion."

"Yes, yes—but thank goodness there is only one Ponsonby! He will come here no more. Oh, dear. Why did you not tell me what a mistake I was making, Alwyn?"

"I did try, Mama. Beginning with the oysters and—"

She went off into another fit of laughing. "Oh! Those oysters of knowledge and pearls of wisdom! We need another quote!"

Her son looked to Prudence. "We shall find one, my dear Mama. Never fear."

"I have it," Prudence said suddenly. "*A Passion for Learning Is a Great Virtue.* It does not have as many letters as the oysters-and-pearls one and will fit nicely upon the cornerstone."

"Where does it come from?" Alwyn inquired.

"I just happened to think of it," Prudence replied. "I suppose you could say that I am the author."

"Splendid!" Lady Agatha applauded. "And—oh, I do think that Cathy deserves a significant reward for her courage and fortitude. Can we not send her to school, improve her station in life?"

Prudence and Alwyn exchanged a look. "She hopes to marry Herrick by autumn."

"Your master builder? Is he a good man?"

"Yes," said Lord Alwyn.

"Does he love her?"

"Yes," said Prudence.

"Then I will provide her dowry. When Cathy leaves our house, she and Herrick will be set for life."

"That would be a happy ending to this curious evening, Mama."

Lady Agatha rose, wheezing slightly. "I will tell her at once."

Chapter Seventeen

With Ponsonby out of the way, Alwyn's relationship with his mother improved overnight. They ceased their bickering almost entirely and turned their attention to the last little details of finishing the Purcell Library.

Alwyn thought now would be as good a time as any to broach the subject of his engagement. The old lady was delighted.

A potential squabble over who was to take the credit for bringing Prudence and Alwyn together was narrowly averted. He gallantly admitted that his dear mama had been solely responsible, that he was a perfect fool for not having figured it out on his own, and that he got his brains entirely from her.

She seemed quite pleased to hear it.

There were no further obstacles to her happiness, Prudence mused. Her own mama had been informed at last of her daughter's engagement, and had promised to visit soon to hear the particulars.

The wedding would not be an extravagant affair—they had politely refused Lady Agatha's generous offer to help. Prudence had only a bit of money left over from her brief employment as Mrs. Motherwit and Alwyn was short of cash as well. A potential client had squandered his promised commission upon the gaming tables, and they would have to wait for another.

But a simple wedding was what Prudence wanted—and what she had always wanted. There was no one she had to dazzle, no one she wanted to impress. All Prudence wanted to see was the man she loved, waiting for her at the altar with joyful hope. If no one but Lady Agatha and Lady Felicia, Cathy and Herrick, Mrs. Dawkins, and Percival were there, so much the better.

Prudence heard the clatter of horses' hooves in the street below and the unmistakable sound of a carriage drawing to a halt. She went to the window and peeped out, not recognizing the equipage or the driver.

A stiff-backed footman in rather shabby livery jumped from the box and held the door open. A slender foot in a narrow shoe came out first, and then the rest of the person inside appeared. It was her mother, clad in silk and a fashionable bonnet.

Lady Felicia squinted up at the house. So she was still too vain to wear spectacles, Prudence noticed. Her mother's china-doll prettiness had not changed much—her face had always had a glazed look, come to think of it. Lady Felicia believed that showing one's emotions led to wrinkles and so she pretended not to have any. Emotions, that is—the wrinkles were carefully powdered.

Prudence had hoped that her mother would wait until just before the wedding to appear, when Lady Felicia could busy herself with the preparations and not find reasons to argue with everyone over every little thing.

Her manservants followed her up the stairs of Purcell House but they carried no luggage. It was clear that Lady Felicia was not planning to stay long. That, coupled with her unannounced arrival, was an ominous sign.

Prudence experienced a sinking feeling.

Lady Felicia stretched out an elegantly gloved hand and tried to ring the bell. Her nearsightedness made her miss it, and that made her cross. She grasped the brass doorknocker and pounded on the door with all her strength.

Prudence heard Broderick answer. Her mother's words were indistinct, but her tone was sharp. The traveling party entered, there was a commotion in the hall when Lady Agatha was informed, and then there was no sound.

She chided herself for not running down. Yet she could not shake an indefinable sense of dread.

Before long, Alwyn knocked on her door and came in without waiting for a proper answer. "My angel! Your mother is here!"

"I know," she said quietly.

"Are you not happy to see her?"

"Of course I am, Alwyn, but—"

"But what? Come, let us go downstairs and welcome her properly!"

Prudence permitted him to drag her by the hand, out the door and down the stairs. He looked about the front hall, but his mama and Lady Felicia were nowhere to be seen.

"Blast! They were here just a moment ago."

"They must have gone into the jungle room," Prudence murmured. She could just imagine what her mama, who prided herself upon having exquisite taste, would have to say about its bizarre décor behind Lady Agatha's back. Lady Felicia, respecting the superior rank of the dowager countess, would be all smiles and politeness to her face, of course.

Broderick opened the door and looked about. "There you are, sir. Your mother requests your presence. And your mother requests yours, Miss Reese."

Alwyn took her arm. "Come. We shall go in together and announce our happy news."

But Lady Felicia seemed anything but happy to see them enter as a couple. "So this is your second son," she said dryly to Lady Agatha. "He is a handsome fellow but has not a feather to fly with, I am sure. Is your first married?"

"No," said Lady Agatha, looking a bit crestfallen. No doubt she had been regaling her unexpected visitor with a proud account of Lord Alwyn's architectural talent. "But as you know, Prudence and Alwyn plan to wed within weeks. I have given them my blessing and I am sure you will do the same."

"Hm." Lady Felicia tapped her foot upon the floor and said nothing more.

"My dear Lady Felicia," the older woman began anxiously, "surely you will—"

"I will not give my consent," Prudence's mama interrupted. "As she is under twenty-one, she must have it or she cannot marry anyone. I have someone else in mind."

"A rich someone, Mama?" Prudence asked. She was trembling with quiet fury.

"Of course. You shall return home with me immediately. There is no need to pack."

"Oh dear! Oh, no, no, no!" cried Lady Agatha. "This is a most unhappy turn of events! Fetch my smelling salts, Alwyn! I do believe I am about to—"

She swooned into a heap upon the carpet. Lady

Felicia merely sniffed. "Does she do that often? She seems to be a rather theatrical sort of person. Not at all the sort of family you would want to marry into, Prudence."

"You are heartless! Heartless! For shame, Mama!"

Lady Felicia looked at Prudence coldly. "I am merely doing what needs to be done. And do not interfere, young man. Or you will be facing legal proceedings that will ruin you and your career."

Alwyn, who was bending over his mama and patting her face, said nothing. Was one of her eyes ever so slightly open—and had he seen a glimmer of a wink? He had. The fainting fit was a sham.

Well, he was not quite sure of the role he was supposed to play in this little drama or his lines but he could improvise as well as the next man. He got to his feet.

"Go!" he thundered, pointing to the door.

Lady Felicia nearly jumped out of her silk gown and dropped her gloves and fan. "Do not address me in that tone of voice, sir! Who do you think you are?"

"I am the master of this house—and you, madam, are not welcome in it!"

Prudence gaped at him. As her mother collected the things she had dropped, he spoke to Prudence soundlessly. She had read his lips once before— could she do so now?

"Alwyn, your mother!"

She is fine. His eyes begged her to believe him. She saw Lady Agatha wave a hand and began to understand.

"But—"

Go with her. He pointed to Lady Felicia.

She had no choice. Her mother caught her by the hand and practically dragged her out the door of the jungle room. Lady Felicia banged into Broderick, who had been listening at the keyhole, and whacked him with her fan.

Prudence took advantage of the confusion to look back at Alwyn.

I shall come for you, my love. He could only mouth the words.

Oh, dear—what did he have in mind? An elopement? Though she had wanted a simple ceremony, Gretna Green was decidedly déclassé. And it was extremely far away from her mother's house.

The Reese women and their servants made a mad dash down the stairs and into the waiting carriage. Her mama pushed and shoved her inside in a most unladylike way, and they drove off into the night.

Chapter Eighteen

Two weeks later . . .

Alwyn had not come for her—and Prudence had been shut up in this dreary house for what felt like forever. Though grand, it seemed sadly shabby to her. No doubt her mother had been unable to keep up appearances and in order to guarantee some income, had hit upon the bizarre scheme of forcing her only unmarried daughter to wed a wealthy man.

Prudence had read of such things, but never, ever, not in her wildest dreams, imagined that such a fate would befall her. Lest she contrive to escape, a grim-faced housekeeper followed her everywhere she went. Prudence felt like a prisoner.

Mrs. Scruggs's beady eyes were always watching. The woman never seemed to sleep.

Prudence was to meet her new fiancé within the hour. According to her jailer—meaning her dear mama—Sir Clermont Humberson was not just rich, he was filthy rich, even if he was only a squire.

The first Sir Humberson had made a fortune in various unsavory ways and the second and third Humbersons had invested it well. Now Clermont Humberson needed a wife to help him spend it. Lady Felicia had volunteered Prudence and flown into a fury when she heard of her engagement to a nobody: Alwyn Purcell, a younger son.

Certainly her true love would keep his promise, Prudence thought, and rescue her from this dreadful situation. She did not know how he would, but she believed in him with all her heart.

Lady Felicia opened Prudence's door without knocking and peered round it, not seeming to see Prudence at first. Heavens, was her mother so nearsighted that she could not make out her grown daughter standing in the middle of the room? Perhaps that interesting fact could be turned to her advantage, thought Prudence, moving toward the door.

Mrs. Scruggs's thin hand caught her arm in a painful grip. "Ye shall not escape!"

"Well said, Scruggs. Bring her down. I suppose she is presentable. Humberson is too drunk to notice what she wears anyway." Her mother left the door open and the housekeeper tightened her grip on Prudence's arm.

Prudence wanted to cry, she wanted to give her tormentors a good drubbing, she wanted to fly away back to London and into Alwyn's arms. . . .

Speaking of Alwyn, was that his face at the window? Whoever it was she had glimpsed through the glass for a fraction of a second disappeared.

She tugged on the housekeeper's ring of keys, which forced Scruggs to look down while Prudence looked up. The face reappeared—and what a dear face it was. Alwyn had come at last!

But what ought she to do? She could not very well escape Mrs. Scruggs's grip without raising a hue and cry. She stared at his lips, hoping he would tell her what to do next—and quickly.

Go with her, he mouthed.

Prudence stopped struggling. The housekeeper muttered an oath as she steered her out the door and down two flights of narrow stairs.

Prudence heard Clermont Humberson's raucous laughter before she saw him. He was evidently well into his cups. Scruggs half-pulled, half-guided her to the parquet floor at the bottom of the last and grandest staircase, where the revolting fellow waited with several of his cronies.

"What ho! Is this my blushing bride? Damned fine gel, Lady Felicia!"

Her dear mama merely nodded, Prudence noticed. Perhaps she too was overcome by the sour smell of strong ale upon his breath.

Humberson belched. "Bring her closer, Scruggs."

The housekeeper obeyed. Prudence was led forth for his inspection. He looked her up and down, and belched again, more loudly. She slapped him, hard.

He laughed uproariously and so did his companions. "She has spirit, I'll give her that! And this!" He gave her a friendly slap upon the rump and Prudence squeaked with outrage. "Damned fine gel!"

Scruggs, fearing the worst, tightened her grip on Prudence as the men went back into the billiard room and resumed their game.

"Mama! Have you gone mad?"

Her mother, finely dressed and tightly corseted though she was, seemed to slump. "No, but we will lose our house and lands to our creditors without Humberson's money. I shall be poor—and I cannot bear that. You must think of others, Prudence. It is a daughter's duty."

She spluttered. "I have never heard such nonsense in my life!"

"But you are very young. Imagine how much nonsense you will have heard by the time you are my age."

"Mama, I am not a prize pig to be sold to the highest bidder!"

Lady Felicia leaned against a column and sighed. "In truth, I had not expected Humberson to behave so crudely. I suppose I am sorry for that much."

"How gracious of you! Now tell this Scruggy person to let go of me!"

Her mother nodded. "Let her go."

Prudence rubbed her sore arm and glared at the housekeeper.

"Now where will you go? You are miles from anywhere and the coachmen will not drive you. No, Prudence, you have no choice. You must and will marry Humberson."

"I shall not! Get my sisters to support you!"

Lady Felicia shrugged. "They will not answer my letters, even though they have me to thank for marrying them off to wealthy men. That left only you."

Prudence put her hands over her ears, unwilling to hear another word. When the housekeeper turned to assist her mother, Prudence seized the chance to gallop up the stairs to her room.

Once inside, she locked the door, then tilted a stout chair against the door so that no one might enter. Mrs. Scruggs certainly had the key. Prudence ran to the window, flung open the sash, and stuck out her head, looking about wildly. There was no sign of Alwyn.

But there was a note stuck in the ivy upon the

wall. She plucked it from its leafy hiding place, unfolded it, and smiled as she read.

Dear Mrs. Motherwit—

I shall come for you by moonlight. Be ready.

Sincerely, Your London Lover

There was nothing to do but wait. She flung herself upon the bed to do just that.

Hours later, she heard a noise. She sat bolt upright. Had she fallen asleep? Moonbeams flooded the room with light and someone was throwing gravel at her window—or rather, through it, since she had not closed it.

Prudence ran to the window, nearly slipping on the little rocks. Percival! She reached out to grab him by the back of his pants and drag him inside but the little scamp managed it on his own.

"Miss, he broke the rain gutter when he tried to climb it. He threw the gravel to wake you and sent me up the trellis instead. He said to tell you I do it all the time."

"That does not mean it is safe, Percival! Still, here you are."

She gave him a hug and only then noticed that he was carrying a tangle of cord that trailed over the windowsill. She rushed back to see Alwyn on the ground, holding a ship's ladder made of heavy rope and stout planks.

"Dearest! Pull it up!" He spoke in an odd sort of thunderous whisper.

"Shouldn't we use knotted bedsheets, Alwyn? Romance heroines always do!"

"Of course not! Bedsheets always break! Do as I say and pull up the ladder!"

Prudence paused. "Have you done this before?"

"No!"

She looked back into the room to see Percival busily untangling the cord. Would the ship's ladder be strong enough to hold them both? She looked out the window at it. Even with the bright moonlight, she could not tell.

"Alwyn, I know that Lady Lascivia preferred bedsheets!"

"Who? Prudence, make haste!"

Percival finished and handed her the cord. She began to pull up the ladder and, when it was in the room, fastened it to the footboard of the bed, knotting the cord tightly around the flexible ladder's first rung. It was fortunate indeed that the bed was massive and ugly, and unlikely to budge an inch.

The ladder was indeed strong enough for her and Percival, if he would allow her to take him into her arms. She could not let him scamper back down by himself, no matter how nimbly he had climbed up.

But before she could explain the plan, Percival straddled the windowsill, swung himself over it and disappeared from sight.

Had the little boy fallen?

He had not. In fact, he was almost on the ground. He landed with a soft thump.

"Prudence! There is not much time! The men in the house are very drunk but they might notice anyway—please hurry!"

She took a deep breath, hoisted her skirts, and got over the sill and onto the top rungs, clutching the side ropes. There was a breeze. Her dress fluttered up to her waist.

"Cover your eyes, Percival," she heard Alwyn whisper.

"Yes, sir."

This was no time to worry about modesty. She began her descent. Truly, it was much less perilous than their climb of a few weeks ago down the library scaffold after sunset. But the difficult situation she was in focused her mind wonderfully. She could swoon in his arms later if she wanted to, she thought.

Alwyn swept her up in his arms before her feet reached the ground.

"Dearest! Herrick is waiting! Mama hired a carriage and a few Bow Street runners to protect us—but we must fly!"

He picked up Percival, whose legs were not long enough for him to keep up, and grabbed Prudence's hand. Running, stumbling, laughing with giddy joy, they soon reached the carriage that waited for them in the road behind a row of hawthorns and scrambled inside, breathless with excitement.

Herrick cracked the whip and they were on their way back to London.

Chapter Nineteen

The morning light came through the stained glass and bathed them all in radiance. The minister cleared his throat.

"Do you, Alwyn Purcell, take this woman to be your lawful wedded wife, to have and to hold, to love and to cherish, from this day forward?"

"Of course. What do you take me for?" He grinned.

The minister frowned. "This is no time for levity, sir. Marriage is a sacred bond." He cast a disapproving look at their torn clothes and tousled hair.

Alwyn made a slight bow. "Indeed it is. Do forgive me. We have had a wild night, as you can see, and—"

Prudence put a finger over his lips.

"Did I give you that dratted paper, by the way?" Alwyn asked the minister. "I thought to procure a special license a week ago, just in case . . . it must be in my pocket . . . ah, here it is!" He brought it forth. "Everything must be entirely legal. For all I know, her mother is in hot pursuit. We must not delay!"

Lady Agatha leafed through a prayer book bound in limp leather. "What comes next? I have lost my place."

Cathy, standing next to Herrick, moved over and tried to help her find it. Percival tugged at her hand. "I am hungry, miss," he whispered. "I had no supper."

"Shh," said Mrs. Dawkins. She looked in her shopping basket for a mite to eat for the poor lad, and found only half a roll she had intended to crumble for the birds. It was stale but it would have to do. The boy took the roll with a nod of thanks.

Mrs. Dawkins gave Alwyn and Prudence a stern look for keeping Percival out long past his bedtime and then softened. How often would the little lad see a wedding like this one, after all?

It was a happy day indeed when true love triumphed. And Lord Alwyn and his pretty bride were the truest lovers her old eyes had ever seen.

More Regency Romance
From Zebra